Voyeur

The Gamer's Girlfriend

Ida Brady

Editing by Hilary Manning
Proofreading by Norma Gambini
Cover design by DAZED Designs
Formatting by Ebony McKenna

www.idabrady.com

To Brian,
For ALL the questions.

To all my Regency romancers out there,
I simply couldn't resist.

Chapter One

Savannah's desire always began in her clit. The tell-tale pulsing, the silent rhythmic throbbing captivated her, holding her in its thrall. Spellbound.

She was learning so much about her sexuality, discovering new kinks and fetishes, finding out what it was that aroused her.

A bit of dom/sub action. Super hot.

Pup play. Super not.

But there was no judgment in her exploration. No shame. Nothing off limits.

Arcas was a generous and open-minded lover. Their sex-life in the past three months had been like unlocking some secret level in a game.

Wondrous, new, and a little fucking scary.

Which was why she was eager and yet nervous as she approached the luxurious estate miles away from the city, about to embark on her first orgy.

The ranch-style home was one of many exclusive properties that dotted the Victorian coastline. Arcas had pointed out the sheer number of convertibles and boutique stores as she drove through Somerton, slowing to a crawl every now and then to gawk at the locals. Every person they spotted seemed to be out of some high-end fashion advertisement. Perfect hair, expensive clothes and a decent fake tan. It was odd and yet fascinating but not enough to distract her from the trepidation that danced along her spine.

Savannah drove through the gated security of the estate and along the winding driveway, secured on either side by large hedgerows. She felt simultaneously comforted and claustrophobic.

Until she spotted the house. It sprawled out in front of them, stretching across the paved drive and extending out farther than she could see. If the grandiosity of the home wasn't enough to make her feel nervous, the sheer newness of this experience did.

She took her time getting out of the car, smoothing down her dress, admiring the plants and flowers. But she couldn't hang out in the driveway forever. Savannah straightened her spine as they approached the front door.

Arcas waited patiently beside her, giving her a light pat on her butt for encouragement. A hell of a lot had changed in three months, including the spectacular success of her online sex blog, 'Sexcapades.' She was fast building up many sexual experiences, which meant a ton of material to write about, not that she could document everything. Lord knew, she tried.

"You know you have to ring the bell to gain entry, right?"

Savannah turned to her boyfriend. His green eyes were bright with mischief.

"I think I'm a little nervous."

"That's totally normal."

"Bec said she'd be coming, right?"

"She did. And that the people who rock up here are legit. It's exclusive and selective. They know about your blog, and that you've got a private channel. It's all above board."

The private channel had been created when a few individuals wanted to take her journaling and sexual experiences to a new level. They'd wanted to watch her have sex online. To see her pleasure herself, making requests in the process.

After chatting with Arcas about the safety measures they would put in place, she had set up an exclusive, private group. Which meant that if anyone actually wanted to watch her orgasm, they could. If they paid.

And boy did they pay.

It had been more popular than she had expected. She was still becoming accustomed to this line of work, not to mention the wonderfully liberating nature of exploring her sexuality with strangers.

Savannah nodded. Drawing in a deep breath, she rang the bell. "It's orgy time."

Chapter Two

One minute she and Arcas were arriving at the stately home, and the next they had been ushered into what Savannah affectionately called the Orgy House. Though without the cringe-worthy washing repair man or a maid dressed in a kinky outfit in the foyer to greet them.

She whispered to Cas, "So, do we need to have rules or something?"

"Try to orgasm as many times as possible?"

"I meant like, are you okay with me kissing other guys? Is there anything you don't feel comfortable with me doing?"

Arcas signaled for her to lean closer. "I've never really been into the two girls one cup business, so other than that, everything goes."

Savannah wrinkled her nose. "That's gross."

"Surely you're not surprised by the internet after all your research?"

"I shouldn't be, but then some new, whacky fetish pops up and I know I can never erase those images."

"Rule 34."

Savannah raised her eyebrows. "Which is?"

"If it exists, there's porn of it."

"Yikes."

Arcas laughed. "Look, I'm fine with you doing whatever you want in whatever way. If you wanna get cocked up to your eyeballs, go for it. So long as you're fine with me doing the same."

"Cock away, Cas."

They entered through the house's double doors and stopped short in the foyer. A wide corridor extended in front of them, with expensive artwork lining the pale walls and a compelling nod to the past in the vintage-esque floral brocade chairs stationed along the tiled hall.

Savannah glanced at the man who admitted them. He bowed slightly, just as an old-fashioned butler would, straight out of the nineteenth century. "Please, make yourselves at home."

To their left and right were two large reception rooms full of people lounging comfortably on plush settees. Some were dressed, some were not, but all engaged in one thing only. Pleasure.

"Bec!" Savannah exclaimed, recognizing one of the women on the settees, her legs spread, a heavyset man licking at her snatch.

"Van, you're here!" Bec leaned down, giving the man a deep-throated kiss before nudging him aside to greet them. She was naked from the waist down, with a light see-through cami draped over her chest. Her dark hair glistened with sweat. "I'm so happy you came!"

"Say that to us in a few hours."

Bec grinned, gesturing for them to follow her. She led them down the corridor, farther into the house. Savannah was captivated. There were paintings of various gods and mortals along the walls, entwined in positions of love, with tamer statues of the pleasure-seeking individuals sprawled around the mansion.

But even Cupid and Psyche's embrace was still arresting.

"Hey, wait." Savannah stopped in front of a room where a man lay sprawled on the ground, and a woman in impossibly high heels walked over his back. "Let me check this out."

"Sure," Bec answered, she and Arcas following her into the room.

The man's face was covered by a leather bondage hood. The rest of him was totally naked. Welts and red marks scoured his back as his Domme balanced on top, holding a silver object in her hands.

"What's that?" Savannah asked, taking a step forward.

"It's a pinwheel."

"It looks like something you'd see at the dentist's office."

The object had a long handle, almost resembling the end of a spoon, but at the tip was a round disc with several short, spiky ends protruding out of it.

"It's good for sensory play," Arcas offered.

"Have you used it before?"

"Actually, no."

"Another addition to my sex box then." Savannah stepped towards the woman. "Is there another one of those?"

The woman jerked her thumb to the table at the far side of the room, where an assortment of items were arranged: ball gags, whips, hoods, ticklers, and cuffs.

Savannah skirted around the couple and picked up the device, surprised by the weight of it in her hand. She walked back to where Arcas waited and sat straight on his lap, adjusting herself without hesitation in her familiar position. A wicked, wanton desire pulsed through her now, as she was emboldened by this new experience.

His eyes darkened as he watched her roll the device over the pads of her fingers, feeling the pressure when she pressed harder.

"You've never been one for waiting."

"Why would I?"

She shivered as the man behind her moaned behind the mask. It was a surprising thrill, knowing that this stranger was getting off on being so bound and restricted. A singing whoosh of the whip against bare flesh, and his moans grew louder.

But all she yearned for were the low, guttural groans of her lover. Arcas. The deep register in his voice when he was lost in his own pleasure.

She ran the device down the length of his arm, watching as he clenched his jaw, gripping her thigh. Savannah trailed it down his chest, around the outline of his nipples through his shirt, then back up, playing with pace and depth.

"That feel good?"

"Mmm."

When she picked up Arcas' hand, his mouth parted.

"What about this?"

He jerked when she ran the wheel from wrist to tip, up and down each finger, until he was panting.

"Fuck, Van."

"That good?"

Arcas leaned his head back, and Savannah smiled. The wet, slick heat in her throbbed, her pussy responding to her lover's passion. The combination of utter submission and pleasure was giddy.

She was a sucker for watching him aroused.

And just like that, she knew that today wouldn't be about her participation. She wanted to watch, to sit back and enjoy Arcas' pleasure with strangers. To greedily take it all in.

"I want to watch you getting fucked," Savannah whispered.

"I aim to please." Arcas captured her mouth, tongue stroking, as his hand slipped between her thighs.

She pressed her breasts against his chest, her nipples impossibly tight. She wanted to rip off her dress and bra, to rid themselves of any barriers to their pleasure.

"I haven't even given you the full tour yet, and you're already settling in like pros," Bec teased.

Savannah broke the kiss, grinning up at their fuck buddy.

"We couldn't help ourselves." She toyed with the pinwheel for a little longer before standing up and placing it back on the table. "But I was just telling Cas I want to watch him get some action."

"Not participating?"

"No, not now that I know what I want."

"Let's go then," Bec answered. "I know exactly where to take you."

Bec's first stop was to an annexed room that resembled a fitness center change area. "They've set up a lock box with a code for any personal affects here. The clothes you can just leave on the bench. And yes, before you ask, Gil and Pen have purposely outfitted this space for their, well . . ."

"Extracurricular activities?" Savannah provided.

"Bingo. But you have to get naked first. At least, Arcas does, if you want him in on the action."

Arcas was already undressing, stripping down to his boxers and shoving his clothes and her bag into the locker.

Bec turned to Savannah. She held a red wristband in her hand.

"What's this?" Savannah frowned.

"Gil and Pen have a system. For voyeurs or first timers not wanting to participate, they get a red wristband. It lets everyone else know that you're off limits, so you don't get approached all the time."

Savannah slipped it on, deciding to keep her dress and heels on as well.

"Okay then, follow me. I think you'll like this room."

Bec led them through the house to another wing, one where the rooms were stately but not ostentatious. Dark mahogany doors opened into rooms with pale furnishings, heavy curtains, and antique-style light fittings.

What would these rooms have looked like in the nineteenth century? How many lovers would have sought the privacy of a darkened room to consummate their desire?

She couldn't help but think about Emmaline and the Duke of Maddern. This place, while modern, held a stately old-world charm. What would Emmaline be doing now? In Savannah's version of *Love and Honor*, she would be travelling to London with her sister, her prospects of marriage a shining beacon on the horizon thanks to her sister's engagement to Lord Fanworth.

She certainly wouldn't be thinking about a certain duke with a skilled tongue.

Savannah quickened her pace, hurrying after Bec as she led them to a room decorated with blush-pink walls and pastoral paintings. It was smaller than the initial reception rooms but still littered with a variety of couples— both on the plush carpet and strewn along the chairs and sofas. Through the French windows, Savannah spied a pool and garden where a few more enjoyed each other and the cool spring day.

Savannah chose a comfortable looking chair and watched as Arcas wheeled himself into the room, nodding as Bec introduced him. It took only seconds for two women, who had been sucking off the heavy-set men on the far side of the room, to extricate themselves and approach. No sooner had Savannah sat down than they had Arcas beside them on the chaise.

"I'm Andrea," Savannah overheard the redhead say. "But everyone calls me Drea."

Savannah bit her lip, trying to relax, to sit back and watch as Bec moved to join the two other men in the room. Kneeling near the French windows, Bec took one of the men in hand and another in her mouth. The fiery redhead—Drea—turned to Arcas, obviously flustered and unsure what to do.

Arcas crooked a finger, a small smile tugging his lips. Oh, how Savannah wanted to be on the receiving end. She could tell Drea was affected by him, and those dark good looks soon dispelled any uncertainty she had.

Arcas patted the seat beside him, running his hand up one thick thigh to her pussy, still glistening from the last person's raid. After a few deft flicks of his fingers, Drea threw her head back, eyes closed as he slowly toyed with her.

Savannah crossed her legs, the heat pooling between her thighs.

She watched in anticipation of what those skilled hands would do next. When he inserted one finger inside of her, Savannah swallowed. The second and third finger disappeared. She was mesmerized by the sight of Drea, legs splayed, head back as Cas' fingers fucked her.

The other woman—with short black hair and tattoos trailing along her torso—shifted closer, inching towards Arcas. She curled around him, sucking and biting his neck.

Arcas slapped her ass, whispering something to her.

Savannah stopped herself from leaning forward, captivated by the low voice, straining to hear the commands he gave. Yearning for that sound he made in the back of his throat when he was aroused.

Mmm.

She could hear it now. The pure male satisfaction at having a woman yield to him.

Lust, as strong as the day she met him, slammed through her.

She wanted to claw at the lucky bitches coiled around him, not out of jealously, but a greedy desire to be fucked by Arcas.

She toyed with her red wristband, a reminder that today's pleasure lay in her perusal. Watching them. Wanting them.

For the first time ever, she realized that Arcas' desire to delay gratification was not dissimilar to the enjoyment she received at watching others. She was a part of and yet separate to their pleasure.

Drea was flushed now, straining against his hand. She heard her protest as Arcas removed his fingers, gripping the tattooed woman by the ass, his muscles rippling as he positioned her, holding her upright, feasting on her pussy.

Tattoo chick squealed, scrambling for purchase. No sooner had he lifted her than Arcas flipped her, so she was bent before him, hands and feet on the couch, the perfect angle for him to tongue fuck her.

Savannah wanted to see his tongue stretch her pussy. The sounds of it were enough of a turn-on as it was.

Savannah tugged at the band at her wrist. She was hot and aching and desperate for a fuck. She craved contact. Heat. The sweet, slick feeling of something inside her.

One of the men by the window, his cock being worked by Bec's capable hands, looked over at her, an invitation in his eyes. Savannah bit her lip. She could have him fucking her in minutes . . .

No. She wanted to toy with her desire more than anything, to stretch the limits of her patience.

She *wanted* to watch as the tattooed woman rocked against Arcas' face, to listen as her cries grew louder. Savannah gasped, spreading her legs. The glorious sounds of Arcas' wet, warm tongue on the woman's snatch drove them both mad.

When the woman came, Savannah's arousal was at breaking point.

It was when Arcas motioned for Drea to sit back down on his lap, facing Savannah, that she had to clench her thighs together. She itched to touch herself, to listen to the delicious throbbing of her clit. She gripped the edge of the chair instead.

Arcas wiped his mouth, green eyes bright. He palmed Drea's heavy tits then tapped at her pussy, toying with her clit, teasing her until she was panting and begging.

He smiled, a possessive, satisfied smile, watching Savannah.

And that's when her control snapped.

She dove her hand beneath her dress, stroking her clit in steady circles, watching her boyfriend finger the curvy redhead on his lap. She imagined herself in that position, with Arcas' hands slipping over her pussy. He rubbed at the pink flesh, and the woman, sprawled against his chest, arched.

Still Arcas watched her, eyes pinning her down.

Savannah felt the flush of her arousal spread through her. She craved him. She yearned for those fingers fucking her, filling her, branding her to him.

"That's it." She watched his lips rather than hearing the sound. "Good girl," he drawled as Drea jerked and writhed. "Come for me."

Savannah felt the heat rise through her body, scorching her skin. Her fingers shook, and she strained with her own need, her heels digging into the carpet, her legs tense.

Just at the point when she was wound tighter in her need than she thought possible, just at the breathless, dizzying moment of surrender, she heard him speak.

"Come," Arcas ordered.

Savannah cried out, flying now into her orgasm. The sparks burst through her, lighting up every nerve, shocking every sense so that she writhed and moaned against the chair, overcome.

Arcas smiled, a grin that marked his satisfaction.

Savannah couldn't wait to take him home and fuck him senseless.

Chapter Three

Emmaline's nipples tightened beneath her silk dress. She should not have attended tonight's ball. In fact, she should never have accepted her aunt's invitation to stay in London at all.

But her aunt, the Duchess of Carrington, could be persuasive. And shrewd.

After Emmaline's run-in with the Duke of Maddern at his estate, her aunt had been commenting on how very gallant he was, and how very attentive he was. To her.

Heaven forbid the Duchess should know of their dalliances.

Emmaline fanned herself. Had there not been the terrible row between Lord Baydon and his wife's lover, they would not have been interrupted.

And she would no longer be a virgin.

She had been in a quivering state ever since and eager to be deflowered. If the carnal delights she had *experienced in his library were any indication of what lovemaking could be, she would be thoroughly satisfied by the Duke's attentions.*

A flush crept over her when she remembered how she had parted her legs for him, how he had encouraged her to seek pleasure on his face, just as his tongue did wicked things. And his hands. And his...

Heavens! The discomfort accompanied her waking hours, an unrelenting, throbbing need that left her unable to control her own desire.

It was a torture too great to endure.

And just like that, her lungs seized. She gripped the fan in front of her face, caught by a pair of glittering eyes across the room.

How many nights had she dreamed to see him again? How many days had she wandered with her sister through the parks of London, hoping in vain to catch sight of him? How many mornings had she sat in her aunt's townhouse, embroidering cushions in the hope he should call upon her? She had begun to think their liaison the product of her fevered imagination.

But no, one look at the Duke dispelled those fears.

Despite the crush, Emmaline felt as if they were the only two people in the room. The music muted, the heavy musk of those around her, diluted. It was the Duke's hands on her body. His Grace's scent on her skin. Above all, the frantic racing of her heart

*that kept her attuned to the one man she would do
well to keep away from.*

The only man to have her heart.

"Emmaline, dear, are you well?"

*Her sister, Anne, was beside her, her grey eyes
filled with concern.*

"Why do you ask?"

*"You look as if you ruined your favorite shawl.
You are quite flushed."*

*"I am well." She patted her sister's arm, sparing
her a glance.*

"But distracted, I see."

*Emmaline turned to Anne. She opened her
mouth to protest but snapped her fan shut instead.
"Am I so very obvious?"*

*"I would say no one was the wiser, dear. Have
you spotted His Grace?"*

*Emmaline had known the moment Maddern
had left the room—her body had stopped shaking un-
controllably. Disappointment sat beside her at his
absence. How she longed to have him close. "No,
never mind."*

*Anne's knowing expression made her sigh. "Do
dance tonight, dear Emmaline. There are many eligible gentlemen in attendance."*

*"I think the Duchess has a skewed view of my
prospects of marriage. I am your spinster elder sister.
A wonderful chaperone but hardly much else."*

*"Tush! You know that is not true. My impending
marriage will put you in the path of very eligible*

gentlemen. And if your confession is true, then the Duke does not seem to think so."

A shiver raced along her chest. She had confessed to her sister the interlude with Maddern in his dressing room but had conveniently left out their dalliance in his study. And the library.

And—

"I thank you for the confidence and the concern, dear sister."

"Refreshments, my sweet?"

Lord Fanworth, dapper in a dark-blue coat, stood before them, a glass in each hand. He was accompanied by their aunt, the Duchess of Carrington, fair in complexion and manner. It was she who had procured invitations for them to attend this ball, hosted by a wealthy young widow newly returned from the Continent. And judging from the squeeze, the ton had turned out in force. Enough eligible gentlemen to make any matchmaking mama's heart dance in delight.

She owed her aunt a great deal for her kindness. Unlike Emmaline's mother who had married a poor barrister, Lady Catherine had caught the eye of the very wealthy and sought-after Duke of Carrington. While her sister, Elizabeth was not permitted in such social circles, the Duchess had ensured that Emmaline and Anne were able to stay with her at every opportunity.

Emmaline smiled, genuinely happy to see her soon-to-be brother-in-law, even if still torn by His

Grace's disappearance. Where had he gone? Why did he not approach?

Her aunt cast a quick look at her before gesturing to a blond-haired man accompanying them. "My dear, I believe you have been introduced to Lord Howard."

"I have, indeed." She curtseyed.

"Miss Collins. It is wonderful to see you look so well. Clearly the Season has been diverting for you."

"It has indeed, my lord. We have been very busy."

"We are kept especially busy by Miss Anne's betrothal, Lord Howard." The Duchess smiled, lines of pleasure fanning out. "Our house is in a right state. Lace and parasols, slippers and day dresses. We are quite overrun."

"But my sister remains ever calm in the chaos."

Lord Howard bowed but kept his gaze on Emmaline.

"Pray, would you do the honor of standing up with me at the next dance?"

Emmaline wavered. She thought of Maddern, his commanding presence and piercing gaze. Where was he now? Why had he not come to ask her to dance?

She was an unmarried woman, that was why, and the Duke's attentions to her were of a private nature. She was foolish to think otherwise.

"I would be honored," she replied to Lord Howard, smiling.

"Wonderful."

And so it was that she danced with a man who smelled like mint and talked of the weather and the number of guests in attendance. He possessed a lively, friendly disposition; indeed, he was charming and attentive. But his eyes did not sear through her gown, burning her flesh and with it her resolve.

She stumbled slightly. Where had he gone? Had he left the ball entirely?

Lord Howard caught her, his arm dipping at her waist, the consummate gentleman.

Emmaline held her breath. Curse the Duke. She was dancing with an esteemed peer. A sweet-tempered earl of good breeding and respectable fortune.

What she should have felt was a trickle of awareness.

What she should have felt was an inkling of desire. Or at least a sense of optimism, of the potential for a secure future.

What she actually felt was . . . nothing.

No heating of the blood, no uncontrollable pulse. Nothing to suggest she was affected by his presence. Or that she wanted anything he offered.

She puffed out a labored breath.

Blast that Duke. Was this what she would have to endure? Would every eligible gentleman fail to measure up to the Duke of Maddern?

Gritting her teeth in a most unladylike manner, she followed Lord Howard through the chassé.

His Grace was entirely at fault. He had conjured

a wicked spell over her. So much so that her body craved his touch. Craved him.

She had no claim on his heart, she reminded herself. No claim on his title. Nothing to bind them as one beside the flesh. And, even then, they had been rudely interrupted.

Why could she not remember how he had jilted her a decade ago? At a time when her heart was tender and impressionable and so entirely his. But her heart had nothing to do with—

There. She could feel it. The familiar tingling at the nape of her neck. An intimate caress that swept across her body, as tantalizing as a lover's kiss. She swallowed now, her pulse unsteady, her throat dry.

The Duke had returned.

Emmaline stumbled again. This time she misplaced her step and fell into Lord Howard's embrace, treading on his feet as she attempted to right herself.

"You are unwell?" Lord Howard asked, concerned.

"I . . . yes . . . no," Emmaline stammered.

"Come. You are surely overheated. Let me find you somewhere to sit away from this crowd."

"Yes . . . thank you," Emmaline replied, the tingling burning through her skin. How was it that it seemed to grow hotter as Lord Howard led her from the dance, toward the inviting refreshment room?

Emmaline fanned her overheated cheeks, needing to compose herself before glancing back. She met the Duke's eyes fleetingly—they seared her soul.

Oh yes, she was very much aware of him.

"Who, pray tell, is that?" Emmaline dared to ask Lord Howard as they exited the ballroom.

"Is what?"

"The woman in the pink silk?"

"Which one? There are many here this evening."

"The one speaking with the Duke of Maddern."

Lord Howard turned, following Emmaline's gaze.

"Oh . . . that is Lady Dewberry. Our hostess. She has been at Convent Garden and the Theatre Royal, but this is the first event she has hosted."

Emmaline felt a sinking sensation growing in her stomach. So Maddern had returned to the ballroom with Lady Dewberry. How did he know her? Were they friends? Lovers? Had they—

"She has been traveling abroad since her husband's death. Rotten luck, to be married and widowed within twelve months."

Emmaline nodded. "I see."

The rolling waves in her stomach drowned out her attempts at reason. Her heart whispered what her head dare not believe. They had appeared comfortable together, Lady Dewberry conversing easily with the Duke. They were a handsome couple, one dark, the other light, with an easy affection clear to all.

"Apparently she goes riding every morning in Hyde Park," Lord Howard was saying as he proffered a glass of champagne. "Quite the . . ."

"Pardon the intrusion."

Emmaline stiffened, gripping the glass.

No. No. No. No.

"Not at all, Maddern. Lady Dewberry, how good to see you! I was just explaining to Miss Collins how you came to be back."

Emmaline turned, curtsying before meeting the Duke's eye. His fierce expression made her want to claw at him.

"It is good to be back on English soil," Lady Dewberry answered. Her voice was light and soft, a hint of a laugh behind it. "And to be amongst friends again. I am so glad you accepted my invitation."

"Let me introduce Miss Collins. She is the Duchess of Carrington's niece. Her sister has just become engaged to Lord Fanworth."

"Miss Collins. A pleasure to meet you. And congratulations to your sister."

Emmaline fixed a polite expression on her face and ignored His Grace's raised eyebrow. "I thank you," she answered. How she did not choke on her words, she did not know. "Your ball is splendid this evening."

She inclined her head to listen to Lady Dewberry's gracious response but struggled to hear it through the pounding in her ears. Her emotions were overwhelming. The Duke was overwhelming. Had he stepped closer? He was so close, so all-consuming, she could scarce breathe.

Emmaline stepped away from him and towards

the safety of Lord Howard and his mint-friendly disposition.

"Heavens!" Lord Howard exclaimed as she faltered against him. He reached out to steady her, knocking the glass she held in her hand.

"Oh!" Emmaline gasped as the near-full glass overturned, sticky-sweet liquid dowsing her bosom and down her dress.

Lady Dewberry gasped; the Duke frowned.

Lord Howard exclaimed in horror, instinctively reaching out to shield Emmaline's bosom.

"Lord Howard!" Maddern berated, censure in his tone.

The fumbling lord soon realized himself, retreating backward as fast as he could.

"A thousand apologies Miss Collins."

Emmaline, mortified, glanced at the Duke, his green eyes bright with an intensity she could not fathom.

"My dear!" interjected Lady Dewberry. "Let me take you somewhere private so you can revive yourself." She led her through the crush, using her fan to shield Emmaline from the most inquisitive eyes. "What an accident, to be sure!"

Emmaline felt the Duke's gaze sear through the back of her gown. She was torn. Why did she feel disappointment when she should have felt relief? "It is quite alright. In truth, it is a vast improvement on the dress."

What did Maddern mean by crowding her in

such a manner? What was that expression in his eyes? She could not place it.

Emmaline followed Lady Dewberry close, admiring the way in which she managed to navigate the crush, not stopping to engage in conversation but, instead, drawing her farther away from prying eyes. She caught a glimpse of a library and a billiards room where a number of gentlemen lounged, before being whisked up the mahogany staircase to Lady Dewberry's own dressing room on the second floor.

Emmaline was grateful for the privacy of the room. The last thing she had wanted was to listen to all the gossiping debutantes prattling away in the retiring room.

"It is too wet to wait for it to dry, I fear," Lady Dewberry commented, indicating Emmaline's dress.

Emmaline looked down, assessing the damage. Her nerves were in disarray, her thoughts overwhelming. She wished only for a few moments alone, to process it all. "You are right. I am quite soaked through."

"You can borrow one of my dresses, if you wish." Lady Dewberry crossed to the closet, opening the door to a bevy of beautiful gowns. "And I shall have it returned to you once it has been cleaned."

"I am sorry, but I am weary."

"I do not doubt it. I shall call for my maid." Lady Dewberry drew from the wardrobe a muslin gown and held it as though to inspect if it would suit. She wrinkled her nose in distaste at Emmaline's current *appearance.* "You really must find a modiste that will flatter your figure, my dear."

Emmaline was shocked.

"But then I suppose I have had the pleasure on my travels of developing a discerning eye for fashion. And for making advantageous matches."

A cold displeasure tickled Emmaline's spine. She longed for solitude.

"Please, Lady Dewberry, do no trouble yourself to call your maid. I am weary and should very much prefer to retire. If you could send word to my aunt to request the carriage?"

Lady Dewberry looked at her, concerned. "If you are certain?"

"Yes. Please, return to your guests and enjoy the evening. If it is not an inconvenience, I shall wait here until it is time to leave."

"Very well. I shall send someone to advise when your carriage is ready. But do consider my advice, Miss Collins. You will enjoy much better prospects if you do." *With a final nod and wan smile at Emmaline's sorry state, she left the room.*

Emmaline, relieved at being alone, went to stand by the fire. She looked once more at her now-ruined gown. It was indeed true. The dress was staid compared to that of Lady Dewberry's. Fair and slight, Lady Dewberry had been the picture of English gentility in her soft pink gown, with her rosy cheeks and small pert nose. It was naturally of the latest fashion, with its high waist and shortened hemline. All that a wealthy widowed could afford while travelling through the Continent.

Emmaline, on the other hand—

Disgusted with her comparisons, Emmaline shook her dress out. She needed to compose herself. And to be as far away from the Duke of Maddern as possible.

"Perhaps you are more comfortable with doing." Maddern's words, once spoken in the close confines of his embrace, brushed over her skin. She shivered at the memory. She was glad to be hidden in Lady Dewberry's dressing room, away from another living soul, if only for a moment. Where she could wait.

Alone. Safe.

Her sense of security satisfied, Emmaline looked around. Here, too, were further examples of what wealth could afford. The tasteful swathes of furnishings, the rich draperies, the plush carpet under foot, all in rose and cream. It signaled Lady Dewberry's comfort and wealth in a splendid fashion. How fine it would be to lounge against the satin-wood sofa, easing her aching feet upon the ottoman by the fire. To simply close her eyes and forget about the ball, Lady Dewberry, or the bloody Duke.

In the opposite corner was a secretaire bookcase, with its writing desk pulled out, teasing Emmaline's curiosity. She crossed to it. What literature did Lady Dewberry read? Was her reading as judgmental as her opinions? Emmaline's fingers traced the ornate decoration on the bookcase before she sat by the secretaire as though to write a letter herself.

What must it be like to be a wealthy widow, able to do as one pleased?

Lady Dewberry was an accomplished lady, and indeed, fortunate to afford such wealth. Emmaline could only imagine the suitors who would seek her out.

Not that Emmaline's chances of securing a husband were high. Not with her outdated evening gowns and dalliances with the Duke. She frowned down at the soaked dress clinging to her skin in the most improper way.

Images of His Grace, on bended knee, face buried between her thighs, assailed her. She should be ashamed of herself, remembering such a wanton act. A proper lady would faint upon such thoughts.

And yet, Emmaline only wanted to repeat it.

She gasped, drawing in a great sobbing breath at the thought of it. She clutched at the confines of her dress, irrationally angry at the sticky gown, wishing to be free of all the confines of her situation.

His Grace had made it very clear ten years ago that a future between them was impossible. If it were not for her aunt's kindness, inviting her to London for the Season, she was certain she would not have seen him again.

Not once in the decade that passed had the Duke sought her company. She received no letters, no invitations, nothing to suggest that he wished to make amends for severing their friendship.

But she was no longer the young girl yearning for the Duke's love and affection. Her mother had sacrificed her own position in society to marry her father, a poor barrister—for love. Emmaline had hoped, in vain, that Maddern would make the same grand gesture. Indeed, she had thought all those summers spent playing as children at her aunt's home had established an understanding between them.

When he had failed to talk of marriage, citing the reasons why they could no longer see each other, she had been crushed.

No, Emmaline's situation had not changed, but her needs had. She would have her pleasure, enjoy the carnal delights of the flesh now, while the opportunity presented itself.

What would she give to have him close to her now? To have his chest pressed against hers? His mouth feasting on her body?

"Blast that blasted Duke!" she muttered, shaking out her dress.

"I do so hope you are not referring to me."

Emmaline turned and gasped. Before she could take a second breath, Maddern closed the door and came to stand before her. His arms, twin bands of steel, reached for her as she stood in haste.

"You!"

"I fear perhaps you were." His voice was low, urgent. "A lady would say thank you. Particularly when I am come to tell her that her carriage is ready."

"How dare you handle me in such a fashion," she rejoined fiercely.

His Grace's eyes glittered, his chest, solid and so wonderfully heavy, pinning her against the secretaire. It was only by the candle burning that she could discern his expression.

Anger?

Surely not.

"How dare I?" He pressed closer still; she felt the steady thump of his heart against her chest. "Has it been so long that you forget, my sweet?" The heavy, thick muscle at her belly spoke volumes.

"Your Grace! Not here! Not where we could be discovered!"

"I doubt it."

But they could be, Emmaline thought. If Lady Dewberry or the maid were to return and discover them thrust up against the furniture as they were, it would be her doom.

"Did you enjoy your dance, Miss Collins?" the Duke continued, his hold upon her still strong.

"I—"

His mouth descended, capturing her, punishing her. He gripped her shoulders and then pulled away, eyes wild.

"Did you enjoy your partner, Emmaline?"

"Wh—"

He feasted on the column of her throat, following the low-cut curve of her gown.

She had yearned for this, for his mouth on her breasts, torturing her, teasing her until she lost control. Until she was half-mad with want.

Emmaline cradled his dark head, running her fingers through his thick hair.

"Sweeter than champagne. Softer than silk," he muttered between bites. "You have not answered."

Emmaline blinked, thoughts in disarray. "Pardon?"

"Did he excite you?"

She frowned. His mouth was beneath the flesh of her ear, his tongue tracing invisible patterns on her overheated skin. Every part of her ached to be marked, consumed, taken by the only man who could overwhelm her.

"Did he tease you?"

When the Duke's hand pressed through her wet skirts, touching her there, Emmaline moaned.

He nudged her legs apart.

"Answer me."

When he gripped her bottom, kneading and teasing, she was consumed. The illicit nature of what she was doing only heightened her arousal.

When she did not answer him, Maddern pulled back. He gripped her chin, his expression as if carved from stone.

"I cannot," she gasped.

His fingers pressed against her mound once

more. She rocked against his hand now, desperate for more contact, silently cursing the fabric of her dress for muting his touch.

She was chasing it. Half-mad from wanting that familiar, clawing sensation deep inside her. The throbbing, heavy ache that seemed only to heighten in his presence.

"I demand it," he commanded across the curve of her shoulder. His teeth bit down, sharp.

Emmaline cried out, pain and arousal scrambling for purchase. "Oh!" She shivered, enjoying the sensation.

The Duke repeated it, harder now.

She bit her lip, attempting to contain her response.

Suddenly, he jerked back, gripping her hips.

"I repeat, answer me."

"Wh—what was the question?"

A smile danced across his mouth. "Did you enjoy your dance?"

Emmaline licked her lips, slowly emerging from her wanton haze. How could she answer such a conceited question?

"I did."

"Did you think of me as he touched you?"

"He prevented my fall."

"Careful now, I am adept at spotting lies."

Emmaline gritted her teeth, blood pounding through her ears. "I did."

"Good. Do you promise to refuse him should he ask again?"

She shifted, lifting her chin. "I do not."

The Duke's eyes turned molten.

Emmaline did not waver. "Perhaps you should have asked me if you wished to secure my attentions, Your Grace. Should the kind and friendly Lord Howard ask me to dance again, I shall certainly not refuse."

She longed to rock against him; his strong hands at her hips held her in place.

The Duke's mouth compressed. Lines of displeasure marked his features. It would have been foreboding. It should have been so, if it had not elicited her own temper.

"Is that so?" His Grace asked ominously.

"As I have said," Emmaline provoked. "Lord Howard was a gentleman. I dare say, if he asks for a waltz, I shall not refuse him."

"A w—" Maddern stepped back. "Devil take you."

Emmaline gripped her dress. This would not do. She could not already miss his touch! "He is well within his rights to ask me to dance, Your Grace."

"We shall see about that," he muttered. "Close your eyes."

"I beg your pardon?"

"Close. Your. Eyes."

Emmaline did so, uncertain of his unreadable expression. How he frustrated her!

She opened one eye just as Maddern maneuvered her away from the secretaire, pushing her instead to the window ledge. Her buttocks pressed hard into the frame's edges even as the draught from the window chilled her soaking dress.

"A disobedient wench, I see." One hand held her tight, and with the other he reached for the curtain tassel, pulling it open, exposing them both.

The anticipation left her breathless.

"What would you have me do, Your Grace?"

His chuckle was low, vibrating through her.

"Obey."

Maddern ran the edge of the curtain tassel along her throat, teasing its way down her bosom.

"What if I cannot?"

The coarse ends tickled her skin. She could imagine His Grace tracing it along the curve of her belly, then lower, torturing her even as he made love.

With a will greater than she possessed, Emmaline kept her eyes closed. Just as with the open curtains, the distant murmur of voices and the rhythmic beat of music from the ballroom below were ever present reminders of their indiscretion. And yet, when she was so very near to the Duke, with the warmth of his chest overwhelmingly close and his masculine scent invading her senses, nothing seemed of consequence.

She gasped when he used his fingernail, drawing meandering, maddening patterns along the exposed swell of her breasts.

Slowly, His Grace lifted her skirts.

Her heart shook.

"If you cannot obey, Miss Collins . . ."

The tassel along her thigh was as unexpected as it was thrilling. The Duke brushed her sex over and again, the soft tickling giving way to an even greater desire.

To be filled.

"Then you will be punished."

His voice was commanding in tone and mesmerizing in its power. Unmatched. Unparalleled. Unrepentant in his effect on her.

Her breathing hitched. The soft brushing of the tassel against her was inexorable.

"What if I dislike the punishment, Your Grace?"

When the pad of his fingertip brushed against her, she cried out, the delicious firmness exactly what she craved.

Unheeding, the Duke pressed his chest against her and spoke low and tight, the message searing her skin.

"I believe it is time you found out."

Chapter Four

Seeking pleasure wasn't just a past time, it was a creed by which she lived.

Biting her lip, Savannah turned on the computer, making her decision.

So what if they had heard her having sex with Cas last month? So what if it was awkward? They were anonymous, faceless whispers over the wires.

Her heart thrummed in her chest; her throat was dry. This was she wanted to do, and she'd be fucked if she let a bunch of strangers make her feel self-conscious about that.

Not that they did. Reports from Arcas were more than favorable about their last session. But he had been with her, sitting beside her, enjoying the fuck-fest just as much as she had.

Tonight, she was alone.

"Guess who's back, bitches?" Savannah said as she joined the gaming guild, adjusting the microphone as she settled into her chair.

She heard someone laugh. It sounded like SnowFlake.

"Welcome back, Van. We thought our fairy healer might have flown away," SnowFlake replied.

"Never. Just recharging my raiding batteries. Did you miss me?"

"We could always do with your wicked skills."

"And what about my other skills?"

There was silence before another person spoke. The screen ID told her it was Lizard344. "Did Cas tell you about our suggestion?"

"He may have mentioned something about an Easter egg." Arcas was away at a gaming convention. He was being interviewed by a few big companies; Savannah hoped the exposure meant he would be in even greater demand when he returned. Even still, it was surprising how much she missed him, regardless of how much they'd been texting back and forth each day.

"And?"

"What's the Easter egg?"

"Are you interested?"

"I don't know. What is it?"

"A sub-world," SnowFlake interjected.

"We'll explain it later. You have to play first. Are you game?" Slayer demanded.

"That's very vague."

"You interested?"

Savannah grinned. "Always."

She could hear Slayer's smile through the speakers. "Let's fuck some shit up then."

Since the last raid, Savannah's skills had improved. While she would never be a tank, and had no real interest in that role, she was quicker and more aware of what the players needed to do to ensure they had a successful raid.

Going in alone, like some white knight, was not going to do the group any favors.

Slayer, in Arcas' absence, discussed their positions then counted them in.

The setting was outside this time, the boss looming in front of a medieval gatehouse, the spikes from his armor glinting with promise.

The blazing fire behind him cast an orange-yellow glow to the courtyard. Tattoos marked his torso, half-human, half-gargoyle, and fangs protruded from his mouth. A menacing foreboding shone from his yellow eyes.

Savannah swallowed.

Was this the fucker they had to annihilate before they reached the Easter egg?

She watched the oversized warrior, his muscles thick and strained in suppressed rage with a heavy battle axe at his side. Oh yeah, they were well and truly screwed. And not in the monster-fucking-good way either.

Savannah kept to her position, healing Slayer as he charged ahead.

They had a good rhythm, and as Slayer knew

the mechanics of the boss, he was able to guide them all to minimize the damage.

Savannah's position was to remain behind a boulder, healing the others as they fought the boss. It protected her from firebombs and axe lunges and made sure she could maximize her healing powers throughout the battle.

But this boss was relentless. She was healing both tanks in tandem and wincing every time their damage dealers took a hit. Which was often.

"When the fuck is this motherfucker gonna die?" Lizard yelled.

"Keep at him. Stick to the plan," Slayer commanded.

Just then, the boss raised his axe, smashing it to the ground.

"This is it!" Slayer ground out. "Move in."

The earth beneath them shook then splintered into smaller fragments. They moved quickly, so as not to fall into the chasm of fire below.

But it meant they were exposed.

"Come at me, you motherfucker." Slayer took another hit, directing the boss to him, while Savannah did her best to heal him.

"Now!" Slayer ordered the damage dealers.

Savannah kept close, watching the players, anticipating the possible damage while keeping a steady nerve. Her blood was up and pumping, but she remained clinical as she studied the position of the healers, the damage dealers, and the boss.

Clinical. Critical. Calm.

"I'm losing my powers," Savannah warned, watching the inevitable depletion. There was only a finite amount of healing she could bestow in any game, and this boss was a skilled motherfucker. Which meant they were taking lots of hits.

"I'm on it," SnowFlake reassured her.

"Shit, shit, shit," Savannah muttered, adrenaline creeping up her spine.

"Keep it fucking steady. We've nearly got him."

And Slayer was right.

They managed to withstand the deafening, ear-splitting roar that tested her healing abilities and debilitated the team, crushing them with its piercing force. She stumbled, in danger of dying herself.

But then, just when she thought they were defeated, the half-human, half-gargoyle boss bastard went down—BOOM—the impact quaking through the earth.

"Let's move," Slayer commanded, leading them all through the gatehouse.

"Fuck me," Savannah muttered. The relief of it was like a post-sex high. The endorphins that rushed through her left her giddy, and all that pent-up adrenaline now rushed out of her.

"Soon," Slayer promised. "Ready for your Easter egg?"

"Fuck yes! So tell me, what is it?"

"A place where your characters can enjoy themselves after killing off such a motherfucking boss."

"Like what?"

"Like somewhere where you can fuck and suck and ride one another while you get off."

Savannah leaned forward, reaching for her glass of water. It was as if someone had said the magic word to unlocking another level of her desire. Not that it was tightly wound up these days, but since her visit to Orgy House, she was on the prowl for something different. An online gangbang? She was all in.

"How does it work?"

"It's like virtual sex thing but with your own voices."

"Yes." Slayer's rich accented voice circled around her desire. "If you're interested, you choose a player, and like animated sex, you both get to fuck each other in any position for as long as you please, except without the fake moaning. We'll get to hear it for real."

"So this would be a virtual gangbang?"

"Yep," Lizard explained. "You can have as many people there as you want. They just had to beat the boss, like we did."

"So, are you interested?" Slayer demanded. His voice was urgent, with the hint of an accent. South American, perhaps? She conjured up images of a dark-skinned man, with long hands and a big, thick cock fucking her until her tits jiggled and her pussy dripped.

Savannah licked her lips. "I'm in."

When the characters on screen walked through the translucent mist into the sub-world, her eyes lit up.

It was a veritable Eden for lovers. Gone were the dark-coloured visuals of death and destruction—the sky was a summer blue, the sun a radiant yellow. The grassy green curves and hills were verdant and lush. And there, on the outer reaches of her vision, were aquamarine rivers snaking through the landscape, shimmering and cool, an invitation for eager lovers.

"We're heading for that hovering castle," Slayer instructed. In the distance was a medieval castle in the sky, connected by thin ropes to the rockface beyond. It was grand and imposing, expanding across the puffy white cloud upon which it sat. Savannah imagined spiral staircases and grand bedchambers. Her clit tingled in anticipation.

It looked like any other gaming world, except for the naked people fucking outdoors.

She spotted a three way by the bushes. Two women were kissing in the stream. A male gangbang was taking place in the sand. On the far side there were fairies fucking dragons, orcs screwing humans . . . all apparently possible. Any position, acceptable.

"You can only hear the party you are with. You can accept randoms to join if you want or keep it tight."

"I'm all for accepting others." Savannah followed close, hovering along the rope line to the castle, her fairy wings fluttering behind her back, breasts heavy.

Inside, there were people on the long banquet style table fucking while devouring food. Cherries and cream were being licked off chests, handles and instruments inserted into orifices. Nothing was truly off-limits.

Arcas' voice drifted in her head. "Rule 34." He wasn't wrong.

"What are the shortcut keys?" she asked.

Slayer sent through the commands. "You'll pick it up pretty quick."

Savannah's heart pummeled in her chest. Her whole body felt alive and buzzing with energy.

Her avatar, despite the fairy wings, was one that she found looked most like her. She had been able to unlock more features in the game, so now her fairy had a fuller figure. Big tits and ass. Round stomach, solid legs.

It was definitely a bonus that she'd been told about this Easter egg. Now she could watch her avatar being fucked and feel like it was her own body.

They crossed the great hall then climbed the stone staircase up a few flights until they reached the private rooms.

Savannah entered the bedchamber with Lizard, Slayer, and SnowFlake, along with a few anonymous users. It was a medieval bedchamber, but grander in size. A large four-poster bed stood in the corner, and a rectangular table and plush chairs and throws were in the other corner for those wanting to get down and dirty.

She couldn't wait.

The heavy throbbing in her clit was enough to leave her squirming.

"You can use the set of commands on the panel to your left to act out certain moves. If you like it, you can set a series of commands for what actions you want to do to one another as well," Slayer instructed. "That way your hands will be free to . . ."

Savannah grinned. "Yes, I see. Like ordering off a menu." She thought about what she wanted and keyed in the first few commands for her avatar. She took that moment to race to her bedroom to get her toys.

She then settled back in the chair, turning on her microphone.

"Hear that sound?" She pressed her vibrator up against the microphone. "That's what I'm going to be using against my clit right now." She did so a few times, circling her snatch, then slid the vibrator inside. She wanted to be totally immersed in virtual sex, pretending she was being fucked by all these different people and creatures. Her vibrator would do the work while she fucked everyone in sight.

"Ready to be plundered?" Lizard asked, his green tail flicking and swishing as he approached.

Before she could do much more than lick her lips, his tail whipped out, grabbing her by the waist, and slammed her on to the four-poster bed.

Her arms and legs became bound by four tentacle-like extensions that jutted from his back.

Savannah was breathless. No sooner had she squirmed against the restriction than she was being pleasured.

Lizard's tongue, an extended forked device, flicked at each of her nipples. She shuddered, as one side was rough, the other soft and smooth. He continued this torture over and over, an unrelenting pressure until she jerked against her bonds.

"The more you tug, the more I get turned on."

"How about you put that reptilian body to use and fuck me," Savannah moaned.

SnowFlake climbed on the bed behind them, taking full advantage of her position of power. SnowFlake straddled her, grinding herself over her pussy, pleasuring them both while Lizard hovered above her tits.

Savannah gasped when his cock appeared, seeming to grow and extend before her eyes. He was heavy and glistening and clearly eager for her to suck him off. Before she knew it, he had split it in two, throwing his lizard head back and groaning.

She took him in her mouth, gagging as his dual-dick hit the back of her throat, pinning her even further on the mattress.

SnowFlake panted, her wet slick snatch fucking her relentlessly.

Van's tits bounced now as the dark-haired SnowFlake took her pleasure, sighing and moaning with every move. She was dripping wet, and unbelievably aroused.

Savannah strained for release but knew it would not come. She was hovering on the tenuous tightrope of desire. Too slow and she would become frustrated. Too quick, and it would be over sooner than expected.

When Lizard reared back and out of her mouth, she gasped for air.

A tingling sensation spread through her, and she lifted her head, glancing across the room to see Slayer sitting back in his chair, watching.

Everyone was lost in their own pleasure. Moans and groans, sighs and growls. All except Slayer. She could only hear his breathing, see his expressionless face as he watched it all, seemingly unphased. It was fucking hot.

When a gargoyle picked up SnowFlake, plucking her off Van's body, Lizard positioned himself. In one hard thrust, he impaled her to the mattress. Savannah jerked, groaning as the dual-dick pummeled her snatch. Like pistons, he moved with relentless ease inside of her.

She bucked and strained against the bands on her arms and legs, desperate to touch, needing only to feel the smooth cool skin that glowed with his satisfaction.

Savannah felt it, the swirling building need inside of her as the cocks fucked her over and over. She was sweating and shuddering, pitching and groaning.

"I need to . . . Oh shit, I'm gonna fucking explode."

"You're so fucking good." Lizard panted. With a feral scream, he threw back his lizard head, his tongue reaching out to slap at Savannah's tits.

And that was when she lost it.

Unable to hold back, she came with such force, she bowed up, jerking and riding the radiating waves of pleasure. Lizard soaked her now, his cum spurting out of her snatch, filling her to the brim, branding her.

Van closed her eyes, letting the fluttering of her heart simmer down to a steady rhythm.

When Lizard released her, she stretched, rubbing at her wrists.

"Fuck," she sighed. Drifting now, she glanced at the few extra people who had joined them.

SnowFlake was having a three way on the far side of the room, a second gargoyle having joined her.

And when her eyes clashed with Slayer, who sat still and motionless, she shivered.

Savannah was about to move when he stood.

"Stay," he commanded.

Savannah froze, watching as he sauntered over. She expected him to cover her body, to kiss and fondle her, but he shifted the wooden chest at the end of the bed, sitting on that instead.

"What would you have me do?"

"Touch yourself."

Savannah bit her lip, running her fingers along her breasts. She inserted her hand in her mouth, sucking on her fingers.

"I want you to take Lizard's cum from your snatch. I want you to lick it off those fingers, really taste him."

Savannah did, taking the slippery green cum, now sticky and thick, into her mouth and tasting it.

"Spread it over your tits."

She did so, enjoying the cool tingling over her body.

"I want you to touch yourself, imagining it's my mouth along your sweet pussy."

Taking her sticky fingers, she circled her clit, already swollen and aching for his touch.

"Is this what you wish?"

"Yes," he muttered, stripping off his clothes and palming his cock. He was a large warrior, built for death and destruction. But here, before her, was a true impaler, that thick cock jutting out made for plundering and pleasure.

Made for her.

"Faster."

She did so, circling her clit frantically, enjoying

that racing, jittery expectation that slid along her body, searching, always searching for that moment of release.

"Stop."

Savannah clenched her hand in a fist, panting.

She leaned against the headboard, her legs parted, awaiting further instruction. Her body was still slick with sweat, and she shivered now at his commanding tone.

"Wait."

His eyes gleamed; her body arched. She ached for release.

"Please," she pleaded, her hand hovering over her.

"You may continue."

Savannah dived at her snatch, rubbing at her clit, building up her desire once more.

She pinched at her tits, rolling the nipples between her fingers as her hand circled her clit. She panted again, feeling the exquisite building. She was so close.

"Stop."

Savannah groaned, taking a few seconds to comply.

"I said, stop."

She did on a shuddering breath, pressing her thighs together.

"That's a good girl."

"How long are you going to tease me like this?"

Slayer smirked, palming his stiff cock. "For as

long as it takes."

Savannah briefly closed her eyes, wanting more. Wanting it all.

He toyed with her, spreading his legs, fisting himself, asking if she would beg for this. Beg for him. Telling her all the ways he would screw her.

And each time she reached the precipice of pleasure, he commanded her to stop. And every time she did, her desire only increased.

By the time he crawled onto the bed to join her, she was a quivering mess. And he didn't muck around.

"On your hands and knees."

She took her time, her own small defiance at being kept waiting.

He slapped her ass to make her hurry up.

In reply, Savannah stuck her ass in the air, kneeling on all fours. The anticipation, the torturous build-up was so fucking hot, she was surprised she didn't come on the spot.

Slayer crouched over her, pausing at her toes, inhaling her scent. He trailed up the back of her thighs, where he hovered a little longer at her ass, his nose brushing at the small of her back then up her spine to her neck.

She shuddered when he whispered against her ear.

"Ready to fuck, fairy?"

She groaned then cried out when he thrust into her.

Slayer hovered behind her, muttering filthy words in her ear, as he snaked one thick hand around her to toy with her clit.

She was a fucking firecracker, burning bright with her need, ready to explode at the slightest pressure. And he rocked inside of her, filling her, fucking her, teasing every inch of her pussy with his thick, hard length.

She tried to pleasure herself, wanting to get off faster, come quicker, but was brushed aside. He toyed with her at first, then worked her in just the way she liked.

Savannah moaned as his balls slapped against her, heavy and demanding. Oh yes, he was just as aroused, just as ready to blow.

And when those fingers fucked her harder and quicker, applying the right pressure, the right speed, there was no stopping that final rush.

Savannah lost all sense of self, both flying out of her body and being caught in every trembling heartbeat, every frayed nerve-ending. And every inch of him. Deep inside.

She sobbed now, calling his name like a chant. Some sacred incantation that would deliver her from her torment. And he did. He delivered the final blows with his cock, engulfing her body with pleasure. Anointing her with his mouth.

And when she came, gloriously hard against his hand, her pussy clenched around the thick cock inside of her, drawing out her pleasure.

"Slayer!"

He tugged her hair, pumping inside her in a frenzy of need, slapping at her ass until she felt him stiffen. His low growl was the sexiest fucking thing, a pleasing rumble that shook every inch of her body.

"Say it." He commanded.

"I'm a good little slut."

"What else?"

She murmured all the dirty phrases now, lost in his pleasure. Slayer pumped his hot seed into her, biting down on her shoulder until he had nothing left to give.

"Good girl," he muttered. "Such a good fucking fairy."

In time, her heart rate evened out and she rested against the firm mattress. Players came and went, but gradually all left, eventually leaving her alone on the bed.

All except one anonymous user.

When she heard his voice, deep and guttural over the line, she smiled, slow and satisfied.

"You've been a very naughty girl, Van."

She leaned up on her elbows. A warrior sat on the chair in the now vacant room.

"Have I?"

"Extremely."

"And what do you think you'll do about that?"

"You'll be punished when I get home."

Savannah bit her lip. She couldn't fucking wait.

Chapter Five

The memory of her soft flesh wet and yielding beneath his fingers accompanied his waking hours. At night, he dreamed of her: her smooth skin receptive to his touch. Her golden-brown hair fanned out across his pillow, and that wicked, wanton expression drove him to commit the most carnal of sins.

Always, Maddern awakened to an empty bed, with an aching in his heart to accompany the one in his loins. How could it be that he still tasted her? That her smell still surrounded him?

She was with him at the club. At the stables. Beside him at the theatre.

He carried her with him, a phantom that taunted his equanimity. So much so that she was fast becoming a part of his life. He sought her out with every waking breath, analyzing his social engagements with a new vigor he had not thought possible.

All because of one woman.

One glance at Lord Howard pawing at her at Lady Dewberry's ball and he had wanted to brand her. Claim her.

Hell and damnation!

Emmaline. He heard her name everywhere he went. Saw her face in every young chit, every bold courtesan. Sought out every opportunity to see her again.

That was why he had gone to Lady Dewberry's ball and to the opera. And now, why he was attending this picnic and not at the races enjoying the company of friends and horseflesh.

A picnic. With more matchmaking mamas and eligible daughters than he would wish.

Maddern glanced across the grass bank to where Miss Collins stood with her sister and aunt. His heart slammed against his chest.

"The nerve . . ."

For there, begging for an introduction from the Duchess of Carrington, was his friend, Lord Walcott.

The debauched and devilish Lord Walcott, the bane of the gentleman's code of honor.

Friends since Oxford, Maddern was nonetheless still happy to give him a good thrashing when he deserved it. And not just with a paddle.

Devil it!

"How very interesting, my lord," he heard Emmaline say, smiling at the new introduction. Maddern's heart twisted. He could not allow that *beautiful, soft face, that sunlight-kissed hair, any-where near Walcott.*

At least, not without him in attendance.

He may have walked away from her a decade before when he was young and foolish, but he would not make that mistake again. He would not be ma-nipulated or persuaded otherwise.

Maddern left his place by Lady Dewberry, crossing to the party.

Damnation, he should never have revealed his intentions to Walcott. He should have known no good would come of it. Walcott liked to always be part of everything around him.

But Maddern's heart had been full, his head fit to explode with all the thoughts crammed into it. Plans for the future. A life greater than merely carousing and gaming.

"*Walcott.*" *He nodded.*

"*Maddern.*" *The sly smile Walcott threw Mad-dern was fleeting, and from Emmaline's serene ex-pression, clearly lost to all others that stood by.*

"*You were not at Lady Dewberry's ball, my lord?*" *Emmaline asked Lord Walcott.*

"*Unfortunately, no.*" *Lord Walcott grinned.* "*I was—ah—otherwise engaged. But I heard it was a resounding success.*"

"*Indeed, it was.*"

Oh yes, a resounding success. In every way.

"*Pray, do you know the Duke of Maddern?*" *Em-maline asked, her parasol twirling behind her. Mad-*

dern noted how she avoided his gaze, color suffusing her cheeks, spanning down past her tantalizing bosom.

Were her nipples hard beneath her pretty dress? Were her thighs wet from remembering his touch?

"Yes," Walcott lamented. "School chums, I am afraid. But pray, Miss Collins, let me show you the small ruins nearby."

Emmaline's eyes brightened. "Are you a historian, then, Lord Walcott?"

"I take an interest. I consider it a past time when I am not managing my estates. But you may even recognize them—Sir William Chambers himself painted them."

"Oh. That does sound very interesting."

"Let me join you," the Duke interposed. "I should not like you to go off alone."

"Of course," Walcott answered. "Let us invite Lady Dewberry to accompany us."

Walcott smiled.

Maddern frowned.

Emmaline stood in the middle.

They were taking a leisurely stroll back from the ruins, the beaming sun searing through Emmaline's dress, when she again noticed that Lady Dewberry had begged for His Grace's attentions. Had her sister and Lord Fanworth not been on this picnic,

she would have feigned a sprained ankle and nursed her fears in solitude. How could it be that her heart was both beating and yet rendered in half?

But try as she might, she was unable to look away. The Duke's very presence left her in agony.

His hard body, pressed against her own.

His expert hands, driving her to madness.

Heavens, she was lost in the memory of their interlude in Lady Dewberry's dressing room.

A mere look from His Grace left her a trembling mess.

But Lady Dewberry's presence doused any daydreams she indulged in, even if Emmaline had tried to dismiss the Duke's attentions to her at the ball. Ever since their liaison, her emotions were as tumultuous as the distant sea.

It had been one week since their dalliance, and she still felt the pulsing ache, the yearning need to be filled between her thighs.

Why had he not come to her? She had expected him to continue their private assignations, but aside from his presence socially, he had not approached her privately.

Emmaline was bitter at being left in such agony. To have to wait for him to send word. To endure her lover's attentions to another.

A titled woman. With money and means.

Unable to block the daggers in her mind, Emmaline glanced at Lord Walcott.

"And how does Lady Dewberry know His Grace?"

When she did not receive an immediate response, she stopped. Her sister, accompanied by Lord Fanworth, were only steps ahead.

Lord Walcott scratched his chin, glancing between the party. "I thought it was common knowledge, but perhaps not."

"Pray, do not keep me in suspense." Emmaline's heart thumped, a foreboding creeping along her skin.

"Lady Dewberry and Maddern . . . well, they, that is to say, they were betrothed."

"Betrothed?" Emmaline could barely hear herself. All the blood had rushed out of her head, pooling at her feet.

"They broke off not long after Maddern's father died. Two years ago, if I am correct."

"And?"

"They parted ways. Beyond that, I do not know," Lord Walcott answered. "I heard there was no objection to the match from either side, so it left her parents in quite a state of confusion."

"I should say," Emmaline forced herself to answer.

Engaged. And recently.

Emmaline trembled.

"But then she married not two months later, so all was forgotten."

What a fool she had been. Here she was pretending that what they had shared was in some way special. Dreaming that it was something more than bedsport when he had actually already chosen bride. His Duchess.

Stupid, Emmaline. So very stupid.

She cared not for this clawing, churning sensation. It raced up her stomach, searing her throat. She feared if she opened her mouth to speak, she would breathe fire.

On unsteady limbs, Emmaline continued along the path, welcoming the cool breeze that bit into her uncovered skin. She was silent, wondering how best to leave. She did not need to feign a megrim—she was verily pained by what she had heard this afternoon.

A pox on the Duke and his duchess.

Tears pricked at her eyes. She sniffed.

She would not be upset over such news. She had wanted to experience carnal pleasure. Indeed, she had entered into such a dalliance knowing there was nothing to be gained. She would not be upset over his choosing a bride so very soon.

Emmaline kept her eyes on the blades of grass, now trodden from their excursion. She had thought they would have more time. Indeed, she was bitterly disappointed that they did not. For she would be no man's mistress, not when he would claim a wife.

"Are you well, dear?" Anne's voice hovered close as the remainder of the picnic party waited for them. She could hear the tinkling laughter of Lady Dewberry still with the Duke.

Oh, how she wished to be alone.

"I am afraid I am not. I need but a moment."
She disengaged her arm from Lord Walcott and turned to take advantage of a well-placed garden seat, a few steps removed from where the party waited.

She had no lingering hopes or expectations. To do so at her age would be folly. But she had not thought this through. Her one goal had been to experience the pleasures of the flesh with the one man whom she had loved, but never had.

"Oh."

She placed her trembling fingers on her lips.

Love.

It was there, pulsing beneath the surface as though she were a besotted young girl and he her first love.

Emmaline blinked away the tears, keeping her head low, should anyone see her cry.

What to do with such emotions? Where to go?

She bit her lip, in agony over her situation.

She was in love with the Duke of Maddern.

Emmaline studied every blade of grass, hoping to control her frantic pulse. She could not succumb to such fervent emotions in present company.

The Duke made no attempt to court her, he made no promises of the future; his interest was purely physical. Loving him did not change her situation. Nor did it alter his feelings. All she could do was withstand it until the end of the Season. She *would reject her aunt's offer to stay on and instead return to her home, back to her parents and the quiet, dull existence that loomed before her.*

In time, she could hope that she might find a suitor. Someone like Lord Howard. A worthy reverend perhaps, or a practical man of means. Or better still, she would endure her life as a spinster, remembering the excitement of this Season while tending to her sister's happy brood.

With a determined nod of her head and a renewed resolution in her heart, Emmaline stood to rejoin the party. Only to freeze as she noticed Lady Dewberry approaching her directly.

The young widow looked the very picture of grace and style. Emmaline wanted only to claw at her in a jealous rage, revenge against the words she had uttered in her dressing room.

"I wished to thank you for your attendance at the ball," Lady Dewberry sweetly said as she approached. "I do so hope your dress was able to be saved."

Emmaline inhaled, horrified. How could she pretend to be so thoughtful?

"Champagne is so bothersome on silk."

"It was well tended. I thank you," Emmaline replied. Beyond that she did not know what to say. How could—

"The Duke speaks very highly of you."

Emmaline frowned. "I beg your pardon?"

"He told me you are both childhood friends."

"Yes. My aunt, the Duchess of Carrington was ever so attentive."

"And now that your sister is newly engaged, I should say such a connection proves advantageous, Miss Collins. Even if your wardrobe is somewhat lacking."

Her spine stiffened. How could she be so bold?

"But let me advise you—you may have not had the advantage of socializing in such circles of late —that—"

"Really, Lady Dewberry, I should—"

"His Grace is a hard man. If you wish to secure his attentions in a more . . . lasting manner, I warn you that your efforts are in vain."

Emmaline gasped, unable to respond. Odious woman! Who was Lady Dewberry to caution her so? When the—

Emmaline pressed her lips together as His Grace approached them.

"Miss Collins. Lady Dewberry. We are all gone to seek refreshments. Please, let me escort you both."

"I thank you, Your Grace." Emmaline curtseyed.

"That sounds quite welcome, Your Grace. I should appreciate that very much." Lady Dewberry flicked her fan, crossing the grass to where Emmaline's sister and the others in the party all gathered for refreshments.

Emmaline stood awkwardly by the Duke. Her heart thumped in her chest. What did Lady Dew-

berry mean to warn her in such a fashion? Had they a private understanding?

"What is the matter?" Maddern murmured, low and close.

"Do not concern yourself with my affairs."

She loved him. She loved him. She loved him.

A dark eyebrow quirked. His lips curled in a sardonic smile.

She wanted to box him. Heavens, she had never a desire to commit violence before. She must have taken leave of her senses.

Emmaline curtseyed again, attempting to leave, only to have him step in her way.

"Your Grace, what is the meaning of this?"

She glanced at the party, lost in their own lively conversations farther along the path. All except one woman. Watching them.

"I would ask the same of you."

"I wish to be alone," she whispered, fury taut in her voice.

His grin turned wolfish. "I can arrange that."

"I believe Lady Dewberry would not wish to be kept waiting."

"Emmaline." Maddern reached out then clenched his fist.

She jerked back. "Pray do not call me by my given name. You have not the right."

"You made no objection when my fingers were teasing your—"

Emmaline gasped. What did he mean to be so bold, with the company only just beyond them?

Maddern clenched his jaw. "Do not be like this, Miss Collins."

"You forget, I am not the one sailing this ship, Your Grace."

"You speak in riddles."

"I bid you and Lady Dewberry all the happiness in the world."

The Duke frowned. "Lady Dewberry and I—"

"Have an understanding."

"Emmaline?" She heard her sister's call. She felt such relief to distance herself from the Duke and return to her sister and aunt.

She could not let this continue. She would be ruined should anyone find out.

"Lady Cowper's masquerade," he called behind her. "I shall send you word. Meet me tonight. Do not delay."

Sexcapades – Sexy RPG

While defeating monsters online can be a thrill, experiencing an RPG style gangbang is even more of a clit stimulator. There is something so very sensual when you can hear another person's pleasure. When you're pretending that you're being fucked and sucked by other avatars in worlds not your own, well . . . it's titillating to say the least.

Here I was, being impaled by a lizard on the four-poster bed, being screwed by a pixie and teased by a warrior all in the comfort of my own home.

So while my character was being fucked and sucked, I was able to spread my legs and bounce on my dildo, using my vibrator for a bit of clit action all at the same time. But it was listening to other people getting off as well that did it for me.

I like the anonymous voyeurism. You don't know what to expect or what commands your other gang-bangers are going to use. It's a role-playing sex-fest with a twist and let me tell you, I'm here for it.

A solid 8/10 on the O-meter.

Yours,

The Gamer's Girlfriend

Chapter Six

Emmaline clutched at her dress.

The low neckline and ruby-red color was as wicked as her plans for this evening.

In fact, the moment she had agreed to accompany the Duke to the Cyprian ball, she had crossed a line. Up until this moment, their dalliance had been secret. Private.

But in attending this infamous ball, she was risking not only her reputation but that of her family.

It seemed she would risk it all.

The Duke's high-handed manner infuriated her still. The arrogant assumption that she would do his bidding kicked up her temper. But still she found she could not refuse him. Not when he suggested the idea, not when a semblance of the young boy, up to no good and mischief, had taken over.

It was not Emmaline Collins, the wanton spinster, that had responded, not entirely. But the teenage girl who had loved so fully, so deeply, that had been called to action.

Now that he had her heart, she was uncertain of refusing him anything.

And the greedy, clawing ache between her thighs propelled her to accept his invitation tonight. She did not care for the consequences of her actions. Only to have him close.

His Grace had organized the logistics like a general off to battle. They had attended Lady Cowper's own soiree not one mile hence, and together they had stolen away. If only for a certain length of time.

"Stay close to me." Maddern's voice tickled the curve of her ear. She looked at him now, his handsome face covered by his mask, his voice the only identifiable feature to give him away.

She cast her eyes away from the bustle of masked men and women entering the public rooms. Fanny Weston, the belle of the demimonde, had almost challenged Lady Cowper by hosting her ball on the very same night as Lady Cowper's own masquerade. Granted, the clientele in attendance did not move necessarily in the same circles, but according to the Duke, it was the Cyprian ball that was the talk of the club. Many men would give up a considerable fortune to be chosen as Fanny's next paramour.

"I do not know where you think I would wander off to, Your Grace."

"And none of that tonight. If you are to address me in public, I am William."

Emmaline felt the intimacy of his request shiver down her spine. "But surely–"

"We maintain the air of anonymity here."

"Even if you should recognize a friend?"

"To single them out in this place would not do. There are rules, Emmaline. And if we are to dance with the devil for one evening, then we must rescind our God-given titles and embrace the revelry."

Emmaline accepted the lick of fear that circled deep in her belly. Despite her recent foray into matters of the flesh, she was still very much a novice. She had heard whispers of such debauchery. Tonight, she wished to explore it further.

That way, when her own dalliance with the Duke came to an end, she could return to her family home and back to her dull and dreary existence as the unmarried firstborn in the Collins clan.

A blush began to form at all she had shared with the Duke. He had unlocked within her a voracious appetite. She was unwilling to starve herself of the delights of the flesh any longer. She wanted to know what it would be like to have him make love to her, to take this torturous teasing to the next stage. If she were to risk it all, she may at least dare some fun.

They entered the Argyle Rooms late in the evening. Emmaline was impressed by the grand pillars and lush green furnishings. But beyond the aesthetic, she was taken by the men and women in various masks and ensembles. Silks and satins, feathers and lace, not to mention the bold and bare bosoms and shoulders on display.

Lady Cowper would condemn such a sight.

Even still, it seemed all the men and women were imbibing to the full. There was an air of freedom and frolicsome fun, the raucous laughter only adding to the merriment.

Maddern offered her a tour, showing her the various open rooms. The rich green furnishings gave way to rooms of opulent fashion. Blues and reds, vibrant settees and plush carpets of the Orient. Every room was different. Every room pulsed and breathed like a living, thriving being. It was seductive and yet sumptuous in the one breath.

Men gathered round card tables; women gossiped in the retiring room and in the farthermost room—the ball was in motion.

Spirits high, the heat almost oppressive, Emmaline was thankful for the Duke's firm hand in hers. The swell of bodies jostling about was as discomforting as it was frightening.

"Come, Emmaline, let us waltz."

She stifled a gasp, shocked. It had only been a threat when she had mentioned Lord Howard.

"But I . . ."

"I shall teach you," he rumbled, his wicked green eyes teasing her behind his black devil mask.

Maddern took her hand and led her to the middle of the room.

She drew in a deep breath, grateful to be away

from the crush but also extremely vulnerable. To be so very close to him, in such a public place, felt too scandalous for even Emmaline's adventurous spirit.

But when his chest brushed against hers, she was lost, unable to refute his offer or the wonder of being intimate in public.

The music, the heat, the triple beat, she was overcome by it all. And the tall, powerful man who held her close. Emmaline had never felt more desirable than she did in that moment.

Tears, hot and bitter, threatened to drown out her joy.

This, all of this, was fleeting.

Like the demimonde and its inhabitants, their relationship was unacceptable. It was not legitimate. It would not last.

The wickedly wonderful experiences she had shared with His Grace would one day cease to exist.

Emmaline closed her eyes, wishing to shut out the melancholia that threatened to take hold. She let herself be carried away in the romance. The dizzying momentum, the whirling movement—she was waltzing. With the Duke. She was caught in his embrace, led by his deft, sure movements. She felt safe in his arms, cradled by his strength.

She allowed herself a few moments to let it sink in before opening her eyes to the world.

When they eventually parted, Emmaline's mouth was dry, and a new, hungry sensation tugged at her senses.

"I think some refreshments are in order," the Duke said authoritatively, guiding her through the room.

Protected by an alcove, he left her there to procure them some drinks. His ever-watchful gaze left her feeling safe in a room full of strangers. Emmaline stood as such, lost in her own thoughts, as she waited for his return.

It took a few minutes to register the woman beside her.

"You must be very important for Maddern to dance a waltz with you, my dear."

Emmaline turned to the woman who approached; her ensemble was as rich and breathtaking as any she had seen this evening. Her dress was bold and, while daring in its design, danced that fine line between decadent and bawdy. Dark tresses coiled at the base of her neck, her silver mask the same daring shade as her dress. And eyes, sharp blue eyes, winked back through her mask.

Whatever happened to anonymity? She hardly knew how to respond.

A warm, open expression caught her now. One that seemed sweet, even if knowledgeable.

Emmaline was struck by the contrast. Where Lady Dewberry, a woman of 'good' breeding, had been snide, here Emmaline found a woman of questionable morals offering her kindness.

The irony of it was not lost on her.

"You need not worry," the woman continued. "I

know everyone's identity here and I am discreet by trade." A wicked curve of the woman's lips put Emmaline at ease.

"I was told to say very little."

"Ah, but that is because you are important to him. I have not seen Maddern bring another woman here. You must be special for him to expose himself in this manner. To share this part of his ... appetites with you."

Emmaline frowned. "I do not understand."

"I have been friends with your darling Duke for many years. He has been a great benefactor to the house I run for fallen women. Those often forced onto the streets by dissolute rakes unable or unwilling to claim their bastards."

"To claim their . . . Pray, excuse me, I do not know your name."

Another smile. "I am your hostess for the evening, though I use that term loosely. May I present myself? I am Fanny Weston."

"Oh!"

"Now the penny drops."

"But how did you . . . Are you and the Duke . . .?"

Fanny inched closer, voice low. "I am afraid I have never had that pleasure. The Duke, for all his scandalous ways, has only ever been a financial benefactor to my cause. And I have never seen him with a woman as I have seen him tonight with you, my dear, if I may be so bold as to say."

Emmaline was shocked and intrigued. Surely Miss Weston was mistaken.

"Do not be afraid to challenge him. He needs a strong woman."

"Miss Weston. I do hope you are not telling untruths to my dance partner here."

Emmaline jumped as Maddern returned. She accepted the cold glass of ratafia he held for her, shuddering as the liquid coated the back of her throat.

Fanny flicked out her fan, waving it in front of her. "Not at all. Merely sharing secret women's business, that is all."

The Duke frowned.

"Your comrade in arms is here, also." Fanny gestured to Maddern. "Having a very good time himself out the back as well."

His Grace downed his glass. "I know it."

Emmaline frowned, confused.

"I am sure you do," Miss Weston continued quite nonplussed. "Nothing escapes your notice. It was lovely to meet you, my dear, but pleasure calls." With a flick of her fan, Fanny left, courting the attention of all the men and women as she did.

"What did she tell you?" the Duke interrogated Emmaline mere seconds later.

Her mouth curved a fraction. "You heard Miss Weston. Secret women's business."

"Is that so?"

Maddern quirked his eyebrow. Emmaline smiled.

"What did she mean, 'out the back'? Is there something more than just the ball?"

His eyebrow steepled further. "Do you truly wish to see?"

"Yes."

"It is secret men's business. It is no sight for a demure lady."

Emmaline held her laughter back. Who was he to comment on whether she was demure? It was he who had seduced her, touching her intimately, wickedly.

"Nonetheless," she insisted. "I should like to see."

"Very well. Then we must return to Lady Cowper's masquerade so that your aunt will not send out a search party. We have been gone long enough already."

Through the reception rooms, past the throng of people, Maddern guided her to what looked like private rooms beyond. It was darker here, not as well lit.

Emmaline was about to protest they should not go farther when she heard it. There, a low murmuring and rhythmic rocking emanated from one of the rooms.

She paused outside its slightly-ajar door, daring to open it a fraction more.

His Grace noticed and smiled. Obligingly, he

nudged the door open farther, so that Emmaline had ample view of the scene before her.

The room was lit by a profusion of candles, the sounds coming from a couple in semi-undress, fornicating on the settee.

She looked up at the pair of heated green eyes beside her, the Duke's expression no longer playful but filled with that very same look that had heated her blood at Lady Dewberry's ball.

Again, he quirked an eyebrow, daring her to look.

And she did. Hesitant at first, but with growing confidence.

The man, his back turned to them, was kneeling, his face hovering close to the woman's sex. Her dress was rolled up to her waist; her breasts, heavy and pink-tipped, were flushed and exposed, her legs parted. Rich brown hair trailed across her bare shoulder. It was a carnal image, an inviting one. Both wore masks, and Emmaline was taken by the revealing nature of their act and the privacy afforded by their concealed faces.

"Do you like what you see?" Maddern moved behind her, murmuring in her ear.

Emmaline dragged in a breath, her own desire ignited by the scene before them.

"Answer me."

"Yes," she replied, amazed at her own response.

In truth, the image of this woman receiving such pleasure shocked and aroused her in equal measure.

Emmaline swallowed, watching as the woman shud-dered and bucked against the man's face.

"Do you wish you were that woman?"

"Y—"

"Or perhaps that man?"

Color flooded her cheeks. Such a suggestion was scandalous. To lie with a woman, to be doing such things. Emmaline was learning that there was much about her desire that she had not understood. Much about her need of which she had not been aware before.

Heart hammering in her chest, she replied boldly, "I do."

Seeing this woman, lush and round, panting in her pleasure, set a need in herself alight. Emmaline wanted to be her. To be him. To absorb the pleasure of man and woman in one.

It was a dizzying revelation. It should have been a sin. Instead, it was a calling.

The man shifted to join the woman on the settee. He lowered the fold of his pantaloons. "Naughty girl." Emmaline heard him mutter. "I want to fuck you before you spend."

Emmaline frowned, a familiarity threading through her mind.

"Please do," the woman replied. "I have been re-miss in my attentions."

She cried out as he plundered into her.

Emmaline jerked as if she had been the woman receiving pleasure. She suppressed a shiver, but in-

stead felt the pulsing ache between her thighs, as strong and powerful as the man standing behind her.

She had never seen a man and woman in amorous congress. It was wanton, wicked. And utterly glorious. She was enraptured by the way his heavy length disappeared inside the woman only to reappear slick and glistening, and so very rigid.

"You wish it were you being plundered," Maddern murmured in her ear. "That it was my cock inside you."

"Oh."

The Duke was close behind her, never touching, never claiming. Instead, he surrounded her with his warmth, his voice burning sinful images in her ear. The darkness of the hall lent their interaction an intimacy that should not have been possible. But the masks, the clandestine position, the dark shadows, all contributed to the illicit nature of their voyeurism.

In reality, she was in a public meeting house, watching two people fornicate. But in the wicked revelry of the Cyprian ball, it all seemed to make sense.

The moaning from inside the room increased in volume. The man pummeled the woman on the sofa, her naked legs now wrapped around his waist. Her cries were a pleasure-thread leading from the room to her own body.

Greedily, Emmaline watched.

Every thrust was torture.

Every moan was pain.

But the whispered lovemaking in her ear was the most punishing of all. Because she was heated and aroused, in need of what she was watching and half-crazed for more.

Her fingers hovered over her mound. She pressed her hand against herself and shuddered.

"Yes, my sweet," Maddern urged.

Emmaline tentatively tapped at the place burning for more contact, frustrated by the confinements of her gown.

The jolt satisfied in the moment, but it was not enough.

"Again," the Duke commanded her.

She swallowed, mouth dry, but did as ordered. This was wicked. Bold. Deliriously freeing.

The man they were watching was marking a rhythm, the woman, close to her own release. Still Emmaline strained, tapping and rubbing against the fabric of her dress.

"More, Emmaline. Faster."

If she turned, would she find him hard and proud?

She was glued to the image before her. Lost in her own arousal.

The woman began panting, faster, ever faster. A keening cry punctuated the space. They could not keep going. How could they keep going? Surely it could not be pleasurable, evidenced by the painful cry the woman made.

Emmaline gasped as the brown-haired woman

shuddered, watching as both man and woman tumbled into their own desire.

Oh, how sinful! How deliciously sinful! Emmaline strained for more, even as the man withdrew, spending his seed over the woman's large breasts. But her own release would not come. Emmaline was caught, aware of where they were, the pressing need to return to Lady Cowper's ball coupled with a desire to be alone with His Grace.

The man planted a kiss on the woman's forehead then laughed.

"Did you enjoy the show, Maddern?" the man called out.

Emmaline's fingers froze.

When the man's blond head turned, she clasped her hands together, pressing them against her stomach.

Maddern's chest rumbled behind her. "Walcott. Always a pleasure."

Chapter Seven

E mmaline was not satisfied. Like a cat in heat, she craved release.

Returning with the Duke to Lady Cowper's ball, she was restless, unable to be still.

She craved the cool breeze on her overheated skin, something beyond the close confines of the carriage.

Damn the Duke. Damn him that he left her unsatisfied. Had that been his wicked intent all along? But why? Why tease her in such a cruel manner?

She recalled the way Lord Walcott had rocked inside the woman. The keening cries that she had — merciful heavens—mistaken for pain had instead been the lady's pleasure.

And now she knew. Now she understood what it was that passed between a man and woman. The very thought of His Grace entering the most private part of her, driving himself inside—she wanted that.

Wanted him.

Fiercely, fervently. Every trembling breath since stepping into the carriage with him had been consumed by thoughts of Maddern.

His expert hands and generous mouth claiming her. His green eyes darkening with pleasure.

She wanted him to commit an act so carnal, it should make her blush.

Lord, forgive me for my sins, she prayed, unable to stop the wicked thoughts that danced through her mind. She craved more.

"Penny for your thoughts?" the Duke interrupted beside her in the carriage. He had divested himself of his mask, protected in the darkened carriage. Emmaline followed suit, turning to face him.

Her heart leapt in her chest, even as her body trembled.

"That . . . He . . ."

"You enjoyed it?"

"Yes."

"You know—I can oblige, my dear Emmaline."

Oh sweet, sweet torture, to have him address her so.

Maddern moved closer to where she sat, stroking her arm upward to her bosom, his eyes ever watchful of her response. Her nipples were aching peaks, sensitive and straining against her evening gown. When he drew her close, pressing her against his hard, firm length, she shuddered.

"You are flushed," he murmured. His voice was thick, low, a tantalizing call.

"I assure you I am well."

"I doubt it not. But you will be better after a tupping, I assure you."

Her breath hitched. She was becoming accustomed to his scandalous speech, welcomed it and its sin.

"I should think you are correct."

She could see his grin was wolfish in the darkness.

But she was no lamb.

Emmaline ran her hands along the bottom of his waistcoat, desiring more. Yearning for more. For him.

"Walcott and I share many things together."

"Perhaps you can educate me."

Emboldened, Emmaline leaned forward, capturing his mouth. She cared not for what was proper. She desired only him.

His hands gripped her waist then traveled with desirous intent up her spine as he gathered her impossibly close. Emmaline's lips curved, even as she gripped his arms, feeling the powerful bands of muscle wind around her.

With him she felt safe.

With him she felt desired.

Loved.

She drew back, the better to see the expression on his face.

He was affected as much as she.

"I want you. I cannot wait."

She was painfully aroused. The heavy aching between her thighs would not abate.

"Nor me."

Maddern hauled her onto his lap, cupping her sex. His voice was low, gravelly, and thick with his arousal. "But I promised you would be punished. Have you forgot?"

He drew up the length of her gown; she felt the torturous shifting of her petticoats as it brushed her calves, then her thighs. His fingers nudged her legs apart as his hand stroked her, toying with her sex.

"You are more than ready."

"Please," she panted, gripping her dress at her waist.

Then froze.

When had the carriage stopped? Why was it no longer moving?

She had no chance to question him, barely stifling a scream as he flipped her on to her stomach to lie across his lap.

Maddern trailed a finger down the curve of her bottom, parting her flesh, inserting himself into the most intimate part of her. She shuddered when he played with her, his arm a band of steel around her waist, keeping her in place.

"Please," she begged a second time, squirming against him.

"This is your punishment." His finger swirled and circled her. Slow, steady strokes until she was straining.

"*Why?*"

"*For dancing with Lord Howard.*"

He aimed a light tap against her soft sex. She jumped, the shock arrowing through her. The air was heavy, the smell of the carriage mingling with her scent.

"*That is not a crime . . . last I—oh! . . . checked Almack's guide t-to ballroom etiquette.*"

"*Impertinent wench.*"

The Duke continued his slow, skilled exploration of her, stroking and seducing until she dug her fingers into his thigh.

"*Hellcat!*"

"*Please! I cannot bear it.*"

"*But you must.*"

She could feel him, hard and pulsing beneath her.

"*It is time I made you mine.*"

His hot mouth planted even hotter kisses along her back, up to her neck. She sighed when he turned her over, nudging her onto the cushions of the carriage seat.

Emmaline's body burned beneath her gown; he tugged down the fabric, gazing at her breasts in appreciation.

"*Do you know how long I have dreamt of this?*"

Her mouth parted, but she knew not what to say. She was caught by him, by that covetous, greedy manner in which he gazed at her. It did something very wicked to her insides. In that look, she could forgive anything.

"Relax your muscles," Maddern coached her as he snaked his hand up her skirts once more, swirling one digit at her entrance.

Emmaline nodded a silent approval, even as she squirmed at the intrusion. He withdrew his finger then placed it in her mouth.

Her eyes rounded.

"Taste yourself. The sweetest of all nectars. This is what pumps the blood in my body. This is what makes me hard. To sample but a taste of you, my sweet . . ."

His Grace inserted the fingers into his own mouth, gathering moisture before inserting a second finger inside her.

Emmaline cried out, gripping his shoulders, burying her head to the side.

He withdrew, murmuring soft, sweet endearments.

The awareness of what they were doing should have had her donning her clothes in shame. "I do not wish for you to stop," she panted.

She ignored the pain in her heart.

Not a duchess. Never his duchess.

Emmaline focused on this new sensation, watching as the Duke parted her thighs, lifting her skirts to find her throbbing and ready.

The brush of his fingers had her stifling a groan.

There. Oh, sweet heavens. There.

With urgency, he divested himself of his clothes until his cravat hung loose about his neck. She snaked her hands underneath his shirt, emboldened by his ragged breathing, the way he claimed her mouth with a brutal passion, a branding desire.

Emmaline sighed at the bands of muscle, the coarse hairs on his chest, before he shifted back, unbuttoning his breeches, freeing himself.

He leaned toward her, rubbing his thick length against her sensitive bud.

Emmaline murmured his name. The Duke. Maddern. The tingling sensation began anew, but still, he did not enter her.

She arched against him, yearning to be filled. She was growing damp between her thighs, wetting his carriage seat beneath them. The yearning inside her turned into a pulsing, aching need.

Still, he kept rocking against her swollen sex.

"Wrap your legs around my waist, my sweet."

She did, shivering at his groan of appreciation.

"You are exquisite. Soft and delicate. And all mine."

His eyes, dazed by his own passion, pierced through her soul. If only the words he spoke were true.

But she was lost in him, in the wicked press of his firm length against her, in the heavy crushing of his chest on her breasts. Emmaline wrapped her arms around him, anchoring him to her. She panted, feeling the familiar longing building inside of her.

The friction of his hard length and the rocking motion against her sex was an exquisite torture.

"*I think you the most beautiful, the most captivating woman I have had the pleasure to meet, Emmaline.*"

The thrill of her name on his lips awoke something unfulfilled inside her.

She strained against him, eager for more.

Maddern shifted himself and positioned her above him, so that she straddled his torso. He spat on his palm, coating himself. She was mesmerized by his jutting sex, proud and stiff between them.

Emmaline worried her lip, suddenly afraid.

"*What if it does not fit?*"

The Duke pressed a hard kiss to her mouth. "Your body will yield to mine, sweet Emmaline. As it was intended."

Tentatively, she sank down upon him, easing his erection inside. No sooner had she begun, than she stopped. Tensed.

He teased her flesh, swirling invisible patterns with his fingers until the burning turned into a dull ache. She tried once more, crying out at the pain.

"*Come to me,*" *Maddern instructed, planting kisses on her mouth. She pressed closer, losing herself in the kiss, until the pressure between her thighs resumed.*

"*Let your womb take me.*"

Emmaline cried out against his mouth, kissing him with a wild, desperate need, shutting her eyes against the drilling pain. Inch by inch, he plundered through her barriers, impaling her.

She was shaking and damp, perspiration moistening her skin.

Taking a deep breath, Emmaline embraced the very experience she had craved for so long. Slowly, ever slowly, she sank down, breathing out until he was buried inside her. Until there was no room to even breathe, for he had claimed her so completely. She was in awe of the wonderous joining between them.

How could such a joyous act be so sinful?

Emmaline panted. The dragging, piercing force of him inside of her was painful, yes, but wonderfully filling.

She watched as he took her fingers in his mouth, moistening it for her to use against herself. She did so, eager and breathless, all reserve fading.

She enjoyed the way Maddern watched her, eyes greedily raking over her heaving bosom. She wanted to experience it all. With him.

"You are mine. All mine," he groaned.

Emmaline lifted her hips, sobbing at the ache, riding him. With every move, the pain hovered close, until only the echoes of it remained. She was lost in the hungry green eyes beneath her, consumed by the arousing words he spoke.

And like that, the discomfort shifted, replaced by a muted pleasure.

Emmaline's fingers flew over herself now, and

with the Duke's guidance, she bounced over him, working herself, searching for that delirium once more.

Maddern reached out for her, gripping her hips.

"My name. Speak it."

Emmaline bit her lip, heart yearning, body straining. She was intoxicated by him, by this need that spurred her on.

With growing confidence, she took her pleasure, and as the slow, soft rising overcame her, she arched back, sobbing, searching, desperate for release.

"Maddern. Your Grace."

"William. Tonight, I am William."

"William."

"Again."

"William . . . oh!"

"Sweet, sweet, Emmaline. Fuck!"

Crying out, she let go, hurtling faster and faster toward that satisfying finish. And when she did, when she tumbled over and over and again, it was glorious and unashamed and everything she had needed.

William was everything she needed.

"Wench! This is what you do to me." He sat up, gripping her waist close, a raw primal burst of passion taking over.

She felt a warmth flooding through her as he pumped, pumped, pumped into her. With a cry, he lifted her as his hot seed spread between them. Emmaline held on, watching in fascination as William *succumbed to his own release, groaning in pleasure.*

Another dress ruined. This one also soaked.

She gripped him close and could hear his heart beating just as hard as hers. It gave her a small satisfaction to hear it.

Society and her lack of fortune meant nothing when in his arms.

William kissed the top of her head and her heart squeezed at the gesture, a glow suffusing her.

"Penny for your thoughts?" he asked again.

Emmaline looked up at him, heat pooling on her cheeks. "You may think I am a wanton."

"Why so?"

"Is it possible to do that again?"

William laughed, his eyes dancing merrily. "I think that is a wonderfully wanton response. One, dear Emmaline, that I am only happy to oblige."

Chapter Eight

Then came the fall.

The very thing that she dreaded had occurred.

Savannah had been found out. Not just found out, but sickeningly vilified by the those who didn't understand her world.

Didn't accept her.

It began with a nasty email. Then the messages bombarding her site.

YOU'RE DEPRAVED.
GOING TO HELL.
WHORE OF BABYLON.
SINNER OF THE FLESH.

Savannah's stomach churned, though she did her best to carry on, to block and delete the comments, to not let them get to her.

Her online blog had turned into more than just

an exploration of sex. It was fast becoming a large part of her life. It had led her to online sex and the wonder of sex work too. To embracing what she loved doing, without shame. Savannah liked the anonymity of pleasuring herself for men and women online. Of touching herself and knowing that there were people wanting to watch her do it.

She didn't know if the men and women were old or young. They were a sea of faceless people, all willing and eager to pay for her to add another experience to her sex challenge, if she was willing to try a few new things.

Her life was full. She kept her job at the library because she loved it and the rest of the time she was able to devote to her sex work. A balance of pleasure and fun, something she could do with purpose. Savannah had finally begun to figure out what she wanted from her life, not what others expected of her.

But then came the text messages, flooding her phone at all hours of the night. She assumed it was her pious brother, Piers, using an anonymous number, and so she blocked him, hoping it would stop.

It did. For a while. Enough for Savannah to breathe.

"Anything?" Cas watched her carefully over breakfast.

"No, like I said, I think it's passed."

Arcas lowered his cup to the table with an audible thump. "I think you're deluding yourself."

"I don't want to talk about it."

She hated that they fought, that because of it, there was a heavy, oppressive weight between them, an invisible pressure tipping the scales of their relationship.

"Why won't you just go down to the station? At least speak to the police about it. Fucking hell, Van, what's it going to take for you to do something to protect yourself?"

"I don't need protection."

Arcas shook his head, jaw clenched. "Do you know how fucking stubborn you're being right now?"

"It's not your place to tell me what to do."

"Hell, Van, it is when you're clearly not able to see straight. It's like you've got these blinders on when it comes to your parents. When are you going to see that they're destroying your life? That they still have some sick hold over you."

"You don't understand."

Savannah's stomach churned. He would never understand.

"Then tell me."

She shook her head, willing the tears to fuck right off.

"I can't fucking help you, Van, if you don't let me in. This—" He motioned between them. "—isn't going to work if you're not going to communicate."

Savannah shrugged then shoved aside her slice of toast, appetite gone.

Minutes later, the front door slammed, and she buried her face in her hands. She didn't want to deal with this. She didn't want to talk about any of it, especially not with Arcas.

That part of her life was painful. Horrid.

She liked the fact that he didn't look at her with pity, that he didn't know. All she wanted to do was forget it ever happened and move on.

Why couldn't he?

With bated breath, Savannah logged on for her next online session, making sure to have her toys ready. Maybe, just maybe, everything would be okay. She had no other choice but to believe it.

Today she was wearing one of her old bartending outfits: short, black skirt and black tank so her tits were on display, her lacy, white bra peeking through.

One of her clients requested white underwear. So tonight, she would deliver.

"Hey everyone," Savannah welcomed them and began with a bit of upskirt action. Taking her vibrator, she sucked the end then twirled it along her nipples, then lower over her clit.

She grinned at the requests to take off her top, so she did slowly, letting her breasts spill out. Savannah pinched her nipples through her bra, loving how hard they were.

"You wanna see my tits?" She shook her head, taking off her underwear instead, slowly removing the scrap of lace down her thighs.

Crawling along her bed, she turned, lifting her skirt so her ass was on display.

Savannah moaned, toying with her hole, knowing how they enjoyed her pleasure. The thought of them watching, listening, getting off because of her kicked up her desire.

Setting down a towel, she moved to the side of the bed where her fuck machine, a new addition to her collection, was waiting. She positioned her camera, then turned it on, knowing full well how hot her tits looked at that angle. She positioned the other camera behind her so they could see her hole.

She leaned against the bed and sighed when she felt the dildo enter her. She was so turned on she didn't need to picture anyone . . . even if her thoughts flew to her nineteenth-century hero, the Duke of Maddern.

What did they use for fucking back then? How would they feel about sex machines like these? She bit her lip as the first wave hit her.

"Fuck, that feels good."

She squeezed her nipples through her bra, raking her hands down her waist. Slapping her clit, she moaned when she heard how wet she was. The moisture increased as she rode the machine, fucking it harder, legs shaking as her body stretched towards her orgasm.

The pressure, the heavy sensation low in her abdomen began and she held on for as long as she could, drawing out every sigh, every moan, knowing that the release would come all too soon.

The build-up was fucking amazing.

In and out, the dildo fucked her, the squelching sounds increasing, wet moisture trickling down her legs. When it did, she cried out in release, just as the first message flashed on the screen, stealing her breath.

WHORE.

Savannah's heart pounded, caught between pleasure and an increasing sense of dread.

What the hell?

She stood, legs shaking, and crawled to the computer.

SLUT.
YOU WILL GET WHAT YOU
DESERVE.

Savannah trembled, eyes glued to the screen.

WATCH YOUR BACK.

She dragged the covers across her flushed and heated skin, an icy chill snaking across her body.

She refused to feel dirty. Nonetheless, guilt trapped any part of reason, holding it prisoner.

She froze in place, watching lines of hatred spew across the chat.

Savannah jerked at the soft whisper.

"What the fuck?"

Arcas had come in. His face was set in fury as he read the messages on the screen.

Before she could blink, he ended the session, cutting the video link. With angry eyes, he copied the content, making a note of the anonymous user all the while talking in soothing, soft tones.

When he touched her foot, she looked at him, eyes obstructed by tears.

She didn't know what to do.

But thankfully, Arcas did.

He scooped her up in his arms, holding her close.

"What's going on, Van?" he murmured comfortingly. She slumped against him and brushed away the tears, uncertain of what to say, how much to reveal, but knowing that this time, it had gone too far.

Chapter Nine

Trauma lived in more than just her mind. It was there in her beating heart as the phone rang. It lived in the aching muscles when she thought about the abuse.

It was in the tears that fell between she and Arcas when she finally drew breath to speak.

An hour later, after accepting a warm cup of tea and her fluffy robe, Savannah sat on the couch beside him.

"You know my parents were pretty religious."

"Zealots is the word that comes to mind."

"They were also really abusive."

Arcas nodded, keeping silent.

Savannah licked her lips, trying to find the words. How did she describe the deprivation? How did she speak of something she had spent years concealing?

"Any digression was met with punishment. For some reason, my parents thought that being a part of the church meant that they had to take everything that was spewed by those pastors as gospel. And those pastors were treated like Jesus reincarnated. It was sickening.

"A lot of those people in the church were lost. Ex drug addicts, alcoholics, and well, you get the picture."

"I do."

Savannah's voice shook as she recounted what she had never spoken before.

"It started off as little things. Being locked in my room then beaten if I dared to disobey. I was made to starve to cleanse my soul of impurities. That was when I went through puberty and had the devil's sin in me."

"Fuck."

"We were surrounded by people who believed in the same principle. So we were indoctrinated from a young age. My parents were supported in it and told they were doing the right thing."

"This is why I hate religion."

"It's not religion that's the problem. It's the people who espouse extremist views."

"Toemayto-tomahto."

Savannah shrugged. "When you're in it, you think it's normal."

"I get the feeling there's more."

"So I told you that there was all this fanfare with pastors and visiting guests and stuff. A pastor from the UK was over for a two-week seminar, and I was asked to help out with printing pamphlets and organizing the boxes of programs. I was twelve. I was one of a dozen kids they asked to be involved. To teach us duty and responsibility."

Arcas gripped her hand. "Van."

She swallowed. "I wasn't raped."

"Fuck."

"He . . ." The bile rose at the back of her throat, her heart constricting from the confession. "He . . . He was in his fifties. I was in the backstage office when he came in. He said he'd noticed me, that I was a chosen child. But if I wanted to cleanse my soul, to stop the devil, I needed to serve him. It was an honor. A great gift me and my family were given to be accepted like this."

"Fuck no."

"Yeah, well . . . for the two weeks he was visiting, he would call me in to 'help.' He told my parents he saw something in me, that my perspective would shape the congregation in the UK, that maybe one day I would follow his lead. At first it was just rubbing at my back, brushing his hand over my chest. I had hit puberty hard. Boobs and butt. I was always mistaken for an older teenager."

Savannah swallowed, starting to shake.

"I'm sorry."

"Not your fault."

"I feel like I need to say it regardless."

Savannah pressed her lips together then continued. "He started putting his hand up the back of my shirt, giving me back rubs, saying, 'Isn't this nice? Doesn't that feel good?'

"I desperately wanted to please my parents, so I just—" Her breathing hitched, a hiccupping sob caught her words. "—oh God, I just nodded, Cas. I feel sick to this day that I just fucking nodded."

"You didn't encourage it. Fuck, Savannah, he was grooming you. The fifty-year-old fuck was grooming an innocent twelve-year-old. You are not to blame."

Still, Savannah shook her head. It was a sickening weight she had carried with her for so long, she knew it wouldn't be easy to shift. How she hated that her stupid desire to please, to be seen as obedient and quiet and all the traits her parents had espoused, had landed her in that mess. That her feelings didn't matter. But that a man's—a sick man's—needs *had*.

"I felt like I was to blame. I mean, my parents were always punishing me for my impurities. I must have been responsible for what happened. My parents never spoke about this stuff to us. I didn't really know. I was so fucking naïve." Her stomach rolled and dived, the queasy, heavy churning inside of her burning now.

"Not. To. Blame." Arcas kissed the tips of her fingers. The gesture never failed to leave her heart a little lighter.

"I get it. It took me years to realize that this wasn't normal," Savannah continued, needing to get it out, to cleanse herself. "He started putting his fingers under my skirt, touching me, making me touch him. I would go home and beg my parents for a shower. I could never scrub him off. And when he tried to kiss me . . ." She bit her lip, lost in the memory, a kid again caught in a set of unfair rules, in a life that didn't fit. "I knew I didn't want him to be my first kiss. How stupid is that? He was touching my body, invading me, and all I could think about was who I wanted to be my first kiss."

"You were a child, Van."

"I knew it was wrong. It made me feel sick and disgusted. I tried to pretend I had a headache, but my parents were adamant this was an honor."

"Did they know?"

Savannah looked up at him. "They found us one evening. I was supposed to be home for a family dinner. I forgot, so they came to get me. He had his dick out, was making me stroke it. I was half-naked." She trembled. "They were furious. They blamed me. That I had the devil in me. That I had been leading him on."

"What the fuck?"

"Remember, I was a chosen child. Of course I was to blame. It wasn't until I got older and went to a regular school not run by zealots that I realized that wasn't right. But I mean, he didn't do it to any of the other kids. Maybe I had? Maybe I was?"

"Bastards."

"I don't think my parents knew what to do.

They became even harsher in their punishments. I had to fast for nearly a month. My teachers thought I was anorexic, so I started skipping school. It was just too much to take. Then my parents decided to home school me."

"What a joke."

"Yep. When I turned sixteen, they convinced me I could be a good Christian girl if I got married. His name was Leo. His family went to the same church as we did. I mean, he was sweet at first. He was my first kiss. But . . ."

"But?"

"He wasn't right in the head."

"What do you mean?"

Savannah shivered, remembering the wild look in his eyes. "He would get into bouts of rage if he saw me talking to another guy. Follow me to make sure I was home.

"At first, I thought he was being protective. I thought that was a good thing. I mean, look at my parents, what great role models they were. But he was toxic. As soon as I finished school, I got out. I planned it all so I wouldn't have to go back, left them a note on the kitchen table and never went back."

"I take it nothing happened to the UK creep?"

"Not that I know of, but I did send a letter to the current pastor before I left, telling them everything. I don't know if anything came of it."

"Just in case you need to hear it again, none of

this is your fault. I'm so fucking angry and sick to think of what you had to go through."

"I appreciate it."

"I'm here for you, Van. I'm always here for you."

Savannah leaned back against the couch. The overwhelming relief of sharing her past, of having him understand, rushed through her. She took comfort from his soothing words, his soft, gentle touch as he gathered her close.

Confessions were exhausting.

"You can't let them harass you again."

"I don't know it's them."

"Your brother, your parents, all the same thing. They're out there thinking it's okay to harass you like that. That's fucked. Look, Van, it's your choice at the end of the day, always yours. But I want to make sure you're okay. And right now, you're being forced to put up with shit you don't deserve."

Van nodded, taking in a cleansing breath. "I think . . . I'm ready to go to the station."

"Fucking A."

Trauma, Savannah reflected as they drove to the station, lived in more than just her mind. It was there in her beating heart any time the phone rang. It lived in her aching muscles when she recalled the abuse.

And it escaped, unrestrained by fear or persecution, in the tears that fell on the day she finally forgave herself.

Sexcapades – An M&M Sandwich

Well, well, well, if we didn't just unlock another kink over the weekend . . . and what a glorious one at that after a hellish month.

I've watched my fair share of porn. In fact, in the last few months, I've probably watched a lot more than I have in my entire life. But never amongst all my viewing had I come across a M&M pairing as fucking HOT as this.

I don't know if it's because it was between my boyfriend and my online lover or just the sheer novelty of the whole thing, but let me tell you, sex friends, I was damn well turned on by all of it.

There is something just so fucking delicious about the energy between two men pleasuring one another. I can only describe it as raw. Elemental. Glorious.

To see that man's cock disappear inside my boyfriend's mouth, to watch them kissing and touching one another made me so utterly aroused.

I had to get myself some cock action ASAP.

Having a threesome where everyone knows each other has its perks, too. They know what to say, and there's a lot of dirty talk. My favorite, if you hadn't already guessed.

Oops, and isn't that another kink? I'm collecting them now.

And when that person knows how to push your buttons, teasing you with commands, ordering you how to touch your body and when, it's pretty damn hot.

I'm wondering if I need another visit to Orgy House. Plenty of material there, lots of cocks to play with, many ready to plunder.

Woe betide, I suppose practice makes perfect.

A 9/10 on the O-meter.

Yours,

The Gamer's Girlfriend

Chapter Ten

B it by bit, as the days passed, Savannah found her rhythm again.

She took some time off work for counselling. She embedded the techniques she learned through therapy to open up to Arcas about all the things she had suppressed for so long. Things she hadn't even realized she had.

Doing so strengthened their relationship, something Savannah hadn't thought possible.

It helped that Arcas didn't treat her any different. Knowing that he carried on, being there in his silent, supportive way when she broke down about yet another thing, was everything she needed.

A month later, Savannah felt ready to get back into her routine. She was starting to feel good about her life again. To feel good about living.

The calls had stopped. The messages dissipated as though none of it had happened.

Her desire had shifted from stolen daydreams while stacking books to tangible, real-life experiences.

She tested it by visiting the Orgy House again.

More men and women.

More orgasms.

More voyeurism.

She had enjoyed her first visit to Orgy House, watching Arcas fucking other women, burying his face in their snatches as they moaned and slithered over him. Naturally, she had gone home that night and fucked him in a frenzy.

But after the threesome with Slayer over the weekend, she wanted to see more of it. She yearned to watch Arcas with other men. Hell, as many men as possible.

And Savannah wasn't going to let what happened when she was twelve dictate what she chose to do at twenty-four.

Still, nothing in her wildest fantasies could have prepared her for what she saw at Orgy House that afternoon.

The first *frisson* of surprise was when the heavy doors opened. There, just as she expected, was the butler to let her in. But today, he was dressed in full livery, complete with coat buckle, breeches, and knee-high stockings.

"Good evening, sir. Madam. Do come in."

Savannah pinched herself. But the man didn't vanish like some apparition. And so, Savannah did the only thing she could do at that point. She stared.

He was an older gentleman, his posture erect, his silver eyes twinkling in mischief. His waistcoat was a dark grey and just as immaculate as the rest of his attire. This time, he really did look every inch a nineteenth-century butler.

"I thank you, Simms."

Savannah turned her bewildered eyes on Arcas, who was brimming with pent-up energy.

"Welcome to Orgy House, my pet. Tonight is the stuff of dreams."

"Arcas."

"Yes?"

The giddy thrill, the rushing pleasure seized her chest, sliding down her thighs. Her mind raced to catch up with her body's desire. She told herself not to cry, even as happy, nervous tears blurred her vision. Savannah trembled, still in shock, following Arcas as he entered.

She hadn't a clue what to say.

Everyone at the Orgy House was dressed in Regency clothes. High-waisted dresses and fluttering fans for the women, fine blue coats and cravats for the men. It made the furnishing of this stately home even more pronounced.

The ornate-carved side chairs, the titillating paintings, even the bold, patterned rugs of the house all seemed to fit even more now that everyone was so handsomely dressed.

The blood pumped through her. The scene was a scintillating call to her most fervent of fantasies.

"Mr Delio. Miss Preston." A maid, dressed entirely inappropriately, approached with two champagne glasses. Her breasts were large, soft, and on full display in her pink gown. Her red hair was curled and coiled behind her head, with ringlets hanging around her face, and every inch of her down to her faux kid boots were Regency issue.

Savannah ran the very real risk of fainting. How fitting.

She grasped the glass, but the maid tutted, taking it from her fingers. She stepped closer to Savannah, tipping the rim of the glass towards her lips. She sipped at the golden liquid, relishing the cooling effect down the back of her throat.

Savannah wanted a cock in her mouth, another stuffed in her snatch. She wanted to be filled and fucked and pummeled.

"I am Drea, my lady."

"Good evening, Drea. I remember you."

The saucy minx bit her pink-glossed lips, brown eyes heating. She stepped closer, their breasts brushing.

She bobbed her curtsey then brushed her lips against Savannah's, a fleeting, feather-light kiss. Savannah trembled, itching to take her the way Arcas had the first time.

"Not so fast, my pet," Arcas interrupted. "We must have you change first."

"This way, m'lady."

Drea ushered them into a smaller room, stopping at the dark chestnut dressing table. Savannah stood before it, catching sight of her own reflection in the mirror. Her cheeks were flushed, her mouth red from gnawing at her lips.

Drea approached.

"Your clothes."

"Oh, sorry." Savannah began to undo the front button of her dress, but Drea's hand stopped her.

"Allow me, miss."

Savannah inhaled, watching as Drea began to unbutton her sundress.

She looked behind her in the mirror, watching another gentleman approach Arcas, similarly helping him to undress. Their eyes locked and a heavy expectant thrill pulsed through her now.

She overheard the man introduce himself as Brandon, and that he would be Arcas' valet should he require anything. Savannah couldn't help but follow Brandon's careful movements, the way his hand paused to stroke Arcas' lips, the way he raked his nails across Arcas' torso. It was electric. Tantalizing. And hot as fucking hell.

Savannah gasped as the back of Drea's fingers trailed down her chest. She circled her now exposed stomach, using her long fingers to stroke and tease her. Drea's head lowered, her tongue trailing a line from her sternum to her navel, blowing on her now-wet skin, making her tremble with more than just nerves.

Drea took her time undressing her, letting the soft cotton flutter to the floor without so much as a word. She circled her body, her hands touching, always touching, stopping to knead the curve of Savannah's ass or to trail a finger over the scrap of lace at Savannah's thighs.

The sheer cotton of Drea's Regency dress, the contrast between them as Savannah stood close to naked made her wetter than she had expected.

She groaned when Drea dipped her head, biting and sucking her breasts through her bra, her heart seizing when the maid stroked her pussy. Twinges of longing pulsed through her.

When she was naked, she looked in the mirror, gasping at Arcas dressed in breeches and a waistcoat. His shirt and cravat were white, a devastating contrast to his dark hair.

Lust, as strong as the ache between her thighs, gripped her whole body now. Glittering green eyes watched her through the mirror, and she wanted to sit on his lap and take her fill. To pretend she was a nineteenth-century woman who was going to be fucked in every way imaginable.

Her feverish mind had already taken over.

The brush of cool fingers against her nipples brought her back to the present. Drea's warm brown eyes gazed up at her as she dressed her in her chemise. Then came the stays. While not very heavy, they were deliciously tight. Savannah waited patiently until she was dressed in a silk gown of palest white. Her soft leather pumps of the same color were comfortable, and her hair, after some time, was bundled up at the nape of her neck in the fashion, as though ready to be presented at Court.

Savannah shifted, unused to the full-length dress, the way the stays pushed her breasts up so prominently. She was not entirely uncomfortable, but it was certainly different. And when the final ribbon was applied to her hair, she swallowed, in awe at the transformation.

"Does it please you?" Drea asked, running a hand down the length of her arm.

"To be dressed like this? Oh yes. But I'm after another experience entirely."

She dragged Drea closer, kissing her glossy mouth, enjoying the way the other woman moaned in excitement.

Tugging down Drea's dress, she sucked one pink nipple, teasing and drawing it in her mouth, taking her sweet time to touch and taste her.

"Does this please you, my lady?" Drea moaned.

"Very much so. But I wish to taste you."

Lifting Drea's skirts, she ran her finger along her mound then parted the thick lips, blowing air on the quivering clit. Shoving her down along the sofa behind them, she ran her fingers along Drea's pussy, toying with her in lazy strokes until the maid bucked beneath her.

"Oh yes."

She lowered herself between her legs, kissing Drea's soft thighs and the light smattering of hairs on Drea's legs. She was natural and bared to her, supple and sweet-smelling. She tantalized her on many levels, but Savannah yearned to hear Drea cry out. To watch those soft breasts bounce as she fucked her.

Savannah lapped now at her clit, small, soft licks, while she gripped her thighs to keep her in place. She increased the pressure, rubbing the pad of her finger along her entrance. She was slick and wet.

Ready for more.

Savannah reared back and fucked her with her tongue, in and out, enjoying the way Drea's thighs sandwiched her head. She gripped the maid's soft ass, burying her face into her now.

She was beyond aroused herself.

Unable to stop the image from forming in her brain, she rose, lifting her own skirts. She straddled Drea now, then carefully lowered herself on to her so that they were joined, flesh to flesh, in the most intimate manner.

Savannah shuddered, the soft wet pussy beneath her was what she had craved since she had taken that first sip of champagne. She rocked now, scissoring the maid, undulating over her in lazy movements.

How many women had indulged themselves like this? How many had sought the soft pleasures of the flesh, the immediate release from their sisterhood, rather than waiting for a man's stiff cock? For marriage?

But women who fucked one another in the nineteenth century were hardly interested in marrying, surely? Or were they all bound by society's rules in the end?

Savannah increased the rhythm, fucking Drea harder now, watching that pink mouth open in pleasure, those breasts bouncing up and down. The clawing, greedy hunger within demanded her attention.

She pinched the maid's nipples, increasing the pressure when she begged for more.

Drea took Savannah's hands so they wrapped around her neck.

"Are you certain?"

Drea smiled back, consenting.

Savannah gripped her neck, gentle at first but harder with every cry. The maid writhed and bucked beneath her, brown eyes closed as she panted and mewled for more, so much more.

When Drea thrashed, shuddering beneath her in climax, Savannah let go of her neck, tweaking her nipples, letting her ride the orgasm to completion. She was very close herself.

"Not so fast."

Through her delirium, it took her a few seconds to register what had happened.

Arcas was before her, brooking no argument.

"I beg your pardon?"

"I never said you could fuck the maid, Miss Preston."

"I can do as I please."

"I think not. You shall be punished for this transgression. Come with me."

"No."

His green eyes glowed. "Richard."

She was plucked in the air by a giant of a man, thick and hard and handsome as Hades.

"Your punishment awaits."

Arcas sat before her, green eyes lusting over her form. Her skirts were lifted, her round ass exposed as the man behind her hovered, awaiting instruction.

"Her tits. They must be free of those infernal lacings." He flicked his wrist, and Richard straightened. Turning her now, he ripped at the side seams, and Savannah's heart leapt at the desecration.

She was also incredibly aroused.

Richard's mouth tugged at the edges of her gown, his torso firm and hard, peeking out beneath his open waistcoat and ripped shirt. Arcas had seen to that.

"Suck on them," he ordered. "I want to hear her scream."

"As you wish," Richard replied. His deep voice slid beneath her clothes, stroking her senses. He grabbed her close.

When his mouth feasted on her heavy breasts, sucking and lapping at her engorged nipples, Savannah did indeed moan.

"Grab her ass. That's a good man. Really make the wench pay for her disobedience."

Savannah sobbed as shocks of pleasure pulsed down her body, rushing at her pussy. Fuck, she was desperate to come. She wanted this hard, muscled tank of a man to pound her. From the bulge in his breeches, she would say he was thick and heavy and would satisfy the aching need very well.

Her pussy was swollen, her mind a whirling dizzy cloud of pleasure.

"Kiss me. I beg of you." Savannah gasped.

"Sir?" Richard stood tall, seeking guidance.

Arcas shook his head.

Savannah almost stamped her foot in frustration.

"Uh-uh, my pet. Punishment is fair and just. You were not allowed to tup that saucy maid."

Savannah turned to face Arcas, chest rising unsteadily. She was in a room full of fucking people and she was being unfairly restricted to one man. And punished for mounting the maid.

"But I want it, sir. You are unjustly cruel."

"You will receive your punishment, Miss Preston. What is more, you will enjoy it."

"Damn you to hell, Arcas."

His laughter was thick and rich. "But I am very much in heaven."

He nodded, and Richard pressed her down, bending her over the table.

"I want your mouth on my cunt." Savannah moaned as Richard lifted her skirts. She looked at Arcas, seeking permission.

Negative.

"May the devil take you!"

Arcas tutted. "You have not an ounce of steel in you, Savannah. I am surprised."

She was trembling and aching and filled with a maddening desire that left her in an agitated state of desperation.

"Please."

He shook his head then motioned for another maid, already half-naked herself, to approach from her chair. She had been kissing another woman but had been watching their interaction with interest.

"On my lap. Legs in the air."

The woman complied, her snatch bared to him.

He spat on his fingers then pushed her back on the settee. Taking his sweet time, he circled her clit, rubbing the flesh until she bucked and writhed.

"Please, Arcas," Savannah moaned. "I am begging you."

Still, he shook his head.

And every curse she knew tumbled out.

Savannah felt the heavy cock behind her, jutting in readiness and pressed against her bottom. Fuck, she wanted to come. Over and over. With every person in every position.

More so, she wanted Arcas to touch her the way he was touching that woman. She yearned for the hot, wet friction, the slapping flesh against flesh. Savannah wanted every groan, every shiver, every inch inside her, pummeling and fucking until she was shaking and spent.

"Tease her," Arcas commanded.

When Richard rubbed his cock up the length of her burning-hot pussy, Savannah sobbed. "Yes."

Her nipples pressed against the table, and her hands gripped the edge. She stood on the tips of her toes, arching for more.

Richard toyed with her snatch, rocking his thick, oh, yes, it was nice and thick, cock along her cunt before moving away.

"Enough. Fuck me, Richard."

"Not until I say," Arcas ordered.

The maid's cries grew louder. She thrashed against Arcas, begging in her own soft way.

"Good girl, that's my sweet pet. You come for me now like the good little slut you are."

"Yes, sir," she moaned.

"See?" His green eyes held Savannah captive. "She isn't a disobedient wench, fucking the other maid without my permission."

"But I am."

Savannah reached now for the manservant walking past. The champagne glasses standing on the salver crashed to the ground. She freed him with desperate shaking fingers, taking him in hand.

His startled cry soon turned into moans.

She pumped at his cock, enjoying the way his body turned rigid, his eyes hot with desire. After only a brief moment of indecision, he gripped her head, face fucking her.

"You will be punished for this!" Arcas called out.

Emmaline stopped sucking cock to reply. "If you won't have him fuck me, I'll find someone who will."

"They all listen to me."

Just as the woman reached her crescendo, Arcas nodded. Savannah gasped as the cock that had been teasing her moments before picked up the pace.

"Fuck!"

The maid's cries hit her pussy. Savannah reached between her legs.

Arcas stopped her.

"Only Richard."

"Go to the devil."

"So you have said."

She sucked off the man in front of her, enjoying

the way he pumped into her mouth, loving being teased at both ends. She swirled her tongue around him, savoring the heavy feeling in her mouth. She sucked him like the bitch in heat she was, rocking back against the cock that teased her now, desperate for him to enter her.

In minutes, the man was coming, jerking and shuddering, his release as glorious as it was sudden. She drank every last salty drop.

"I couldn't hold back."

"You will next time."

Savannah wiped at her lip then groaned, straining back against the giant who was rubbing at her swollen clit, sending shooting sparks through her overheated body. "Ohh, he's so fucking big."

"And you'll take every inch."

Richard grunted behind her. She heard the lube being applied then watched over her shoulder as he rubbed it up and down his shaft.

He was bigger than she had welcomed in a very long time, longer too. She breathed out when she felt him nudge at her pussy, preparing herself. Inch by inch, he impaled her, stretching her snatch, making her gasp at the intrusion.

Fuck, he *was* big.

Savannah shuddered, panting, and for a split second, she wasn't sure she could handle it. It was almost painful when he buried himself deep inside of her.

And still, he wasn't all the way in.

But she did, instructing him how deep to go, how much she wanted. Thrust by thrust, she drenched his cock as he hit that sweet spot inside of her, fucking her nice and slow, even though she wanted it wild.

Her tits bounced, nipples brushing against the now-warm wooden table. What she would give to have Arcas sucking her nipples, his hands on her clit.

"Ohh, fuck me."

His grunting pleasure turned her on. The sounds of the others in the room was a sweet melody to her desire.

Savannah watched the people around them, all in states of undress, fucking and sucking one another. It was a symphony of pleasure, a sensory delight: men with breeches at their ankles buggering one another, women with skirts raised, face fucking.

And her tormentor sitting opposite, speaking words of praise to the little maid who had come over his hand.

So she took her fill, branding the images before her to memory. Hiking her knee on the table, Savannah changed the angle of the fuck, so with every few strokes, her clit brushed at the wood, driving her closer to that dizzying release.

This was what she had dreamed of. This was the fucking pinnacle of her desire. A thick cock in her snatch, others fucking around her, and the one man who had her heart watching with a dark and satisfying expression on his face.

When Arcas' valet, Brandon, approached her boyfriend, kneeling before him, Savannah groaned. He gripped Arcas' hand then slowly took his fingers in his mouth, sucking each digit.

When Arcas tugged Brandon's hair back then looked at Savannah, she nodded, understanding his silent request.

"Ohhhhh," she sighed, watching them kiss. The masculine energy, the fierce, powerful dueling of tongues kicked up her desire. But still she kept her orgasm at bay.

She watched as Brandon stood, unbuttoning his breeches. His cock was thin and long. Arcas took him in hand, pumping him with easy, assured strokes. It wasn't long before Brandon's cock disappeared into Arcas' mouth, his dark head thrown back, muscles rippling as he thrust inside her lover.

Fuck, that was hot.

Brandon gripped Arcas' head, pumping into him, his ass flexing as he groaned, straining for more. Her boyfriend had a silver tongue after all.

When Brandon took Arcas' fingers in his mouth once more, she knew she wouldn't last. His low growls of pleasure, the energy of them fucking was almost too much to bear.

They watched one another now, both being pleasured, connected but separate across the room.

And when the rising rushing feeling overwhelmed her, gripping at her, clawing its way through her valiant attempts to hold off, Savannah sobbed his name.

"Arcas! Fuck me. Yes."

He threw his head back, body jerking, letting go as he orgasmed.

As did she.

Savannah spasmed around the thick cock inside of her, feeling the trickling wetness running down her legs as she squirted from the deep pressure. It spread through her, circling around her snatch to her clit. She rode the cock now, drawing out her orgasm, sobbing as he pounded her, riding her hard, his balls slapping against her until she begged for him to stop.

Richard turned her over on the table, and in a few strokes of his hand, he came over her tits, hot silky jets of cum. Still her pussy pulsed, wet and throbbing from his intrusion. Fuck. With her dress stained and her body thrumming, Savannah was in heaven.

She turned to face Arcas and grinned. By the looks of it, he was too.

How was it that she was already thinking about fucking again?

And it was just the beginning.

It was a few days later as she curled up in bed, a mug of cocoa and a heat pack at her abdomen, that Savannah put her thoughts to words.

She was still aching from their fuck-fest, with every erogenous zone she thought she had still lit up.

Sexcapades – Orgy-tastic

If I thought I had a good handle on what made me come faster than a bitch in heat, I was sorely mistaken. Because watching and participating in a room full of people fucking is like my very own personal porno come to life. But a room full of people getting their O-on, dressed in Regency clothes? THAT was fucking AHHHMAZZZING.

I understand the appeal of it now. In fact, I'm already wondering when I can try out the different rooms. Tie me up, fuck me down. Cosplay. Even a bit more harness action is on the cards. Though sadly, it won't be in Regency costume. Boyfriend did a killer job making that kink come to life.

The sound of men and women fucking—the slapping, wet noises, the groaning and panting. . . Fuck, I'm getting turned on again just thinking about it.

What drove me wilder than tribbing (though that was fucking hot) was being fucked while watching my man suck cock. There is just something so damn sexy about guys touching each other.

The way he looked at me being fucked, the way he commanded the tank behind me to touch me, well, it made the experience so much hotter. I was one orgy-gasm away from losing my mind.

A definite 10/10 on the O-meter.

Yours,

The Gamer's Girlfriend

Want to find out what happens next?

Read Vixen, Book 3 in The Gamer's Girlfriend Series.

Also By Ida Brady

The Gamer's Girlfriend Series

Book 1

Virtue

Book 2

Voyeur

Book 3

Vixen

Teacher Chronicles Series

Before You Were Mine

When You Were Mine

If You Were Mine (Coming 2023)

A Sweet, Sexy, Scandalous Series

Sweet Spot

Sex and the Stage

Secrets and Scandals

Standalones

To Tango with Love

About the Author

Ida Brady writes contemporary romance novels that promise humour, heartbreak and a happily ever after. With all the sexy bits! A lover of chocolate (milk or dark) and thunderstorms (the bigger the better), she's usually dreaming about her next cast of characters or what she's going to eat for her next meal. When she isn't trying to tame her intractable curls, she's running after her kids, usually with a book in hand.

Ida lives in Melbourne with her Irish husband and their out-of-control collection of books. She sometimes daydreams about having a huge library in her apartment but will settle for stacking novels in the kitchen drawers instead. In her past life, she taught VCE Literature and English to a gaggle of teenagers. While she misses their enthusiasm, she sure as hell doesn't miss marking papers. You might find her dancing the sexy Argentine tango in her spare time, which isn't very often these days. She loves travelling with her family, observing strangers at café's, and getting lost in a good story.
Want to hear more?
Visit: http://www.idabrady.com or sign up to my

Newsletter, With You in Romance for giveaways
and prizes!
Follow me on Tiktok, Facebook! and Instagram or
leave a review on Goodreads.

SUBSCRIBE FOR ALL THE NEWS!
If you want exclusive access to giveaways, sales, and
new release alerts first, then subscribe to my
monthly newsletter, With You in Romance at
www.idabrady.com

Acknowledgments

I am so damn happy to have book 2 out in the world. I have had a hell of a year of illnesses so to get to this stage, where I'm able to share this story with you, is such a relief. I absolutely love these couples, writing them has been such a joy, and I couldn't have reached this stage without my amazing support team. So to all who have encouraged me and shown an interest in this series, thank you times a million!

To Team Brida: Brian, Adria, Niamh and Hugo. I can say I'm the luckiest woman in the world to have you all in my corner. All that love and support, not to mention sweet little hugs, have kept this sleep-deprived mamma going when some days it was just bloody tough. Love you all to the moon and back!

To Hilary, my Alpha reader, editor and friend. I know, without a shadow of a doubt, that this series wouldn't be where it is today without your brutally honest feedback. BDSM style! Your passion for this series has kept me on track so many times when I questioned myself and I cannot thank you enough for all the time you've spent editing and advising me. Can't wait to celebrate with you!

To Norma Gambini, you remain a treasure to work

with. Thank you so much for your editing prowess. I'm so luck that I get to work with you. Like I always say, you're the best!

To Tash, a million thank yous for all the wonderful work on my covers. I cannot gush over them enough. You have a gift!!

To Ebony, formatter guru and all-around awesome person. Thanks SO much for all your work over the years. You're a gem to work with and an absolute life-saver on those deadlines.

To my family, as always for the love and support both near and across the wild Atlantic.

To my wonderful writer friends, my Meetup girls, your advice, feedback and general support really makes me feel like I can do this. I wouldn't be where I am without your friendship and support, so thank you! Here's to another release, and hopefully another retreat down the track!

To my BETA readers, once again, your time, effort and insight make me feel super lucky to have you all in my life. Thank you for all the feedback, encouragement, and support. Y'all ROCK!

Finally, to my readers. Whoever you are, wherever you may be, I hope that this novel gives you a chance to escape from reality, even if for a chapter or two.

With you in romance,
Ida Brady

www.ingramcontent.com/pod-product-compliance
Lightning Source LLC
Chambersburg PA
CBHW030412120726
47904CB00007B/2249